STRANGE MANSION
Tony Rook

When Major 'Freddy' Forbes is found dead down the well at Cold Beech Villa, his pockets stuffed with small coins, foul play seems certain. Inspector Ken Harris, of the Broadshire County Constabulary, helped by amateur archaeologist Peter Wood, is faced with the problem of who might have visited the Villa at dead of night, and why did the Major end up at the bottom of the well.

Forbes was last seen alive by members of the Broadshire Archaeological, Antiquarian and Architectural Society at a meeting held on the evening of his death. Although these highly respectable members of the 'County' set seem unlikely suspects, when Harris and Wood start their enquiries it becomes obvious that motives may include professional jealousy—and envy.

Exhaustive investigations prove inconclusive and it is several months before an article in a learned archaeological journal puts Peter Wood on the trail that finally leads to the solution of the Major's death.

Strange mansion is a thriller packed full of fascinating detail which keeps the reader puzzled until the final denouement.

STRANGE MANSION

Tony Rook

The sages say, Dame Truth delights to dwell
(Strange Mansion!) in the bottom of a well:
Questions are then the Windlass and the Rope
That pull the grave old Gentlewoman up.

John Wolcot—Birthday Ode.

MILTON HOUSE BOOKS

MILTON HOUSE BOOKS
The Dolphin Publishing Co. Limited
at the Sign of the Dolphin
Milton Road, Aylesbury, HP21 7TH
England.

Editorial 26 Parkway, London NW1

First Milton House Edition 1974

*All characters and events in this novel,
except those of a definitely historical
nature, are fictitious.*

ISBN 0 85940 065 4

Printed in Great Britain by Alden & Mowbray Ltd
at the Alden Press, Oxford

CONTENTS

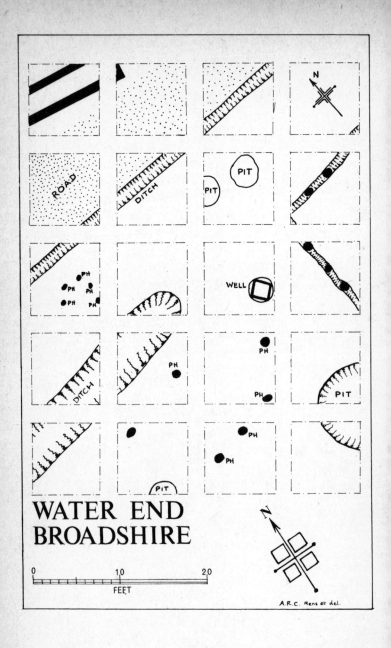

WATER END
BROADSHIRE

0   10   20
FEET

A.R.C. Mens et del.

CHAPTER 1

Known to the police

Peter Wood was an amateur archaeologist. To many people, this description will immediately suggest that he spent much of his time sitting in front of the fire reading of the exploits of Schliemann or Howard Carter, or deciphering hieroglyphics. Such an impression must be countered at the outset. To an archaeologist like Peter, the term 'archaeology' was almost synonymous with 'digging'. He did not neglect his books, but his spare time during the hours of daylight was generally spent in holes in the ground. Sometimes the holes were made by Peter and his friends according to some preconceived plan, to solve some archaeological problem. More frequently the holes were made by a building contractor, and Peter would be allowed a brief time in which to extract objects from the soil before foundations were laid.

It was quite obvious to most of Peter's neighbours that the material taken from the ground with great pains, physical exertion, and risk to life and limb, was just a load of old rubbish. Most people cannot believe that the collection of old bones and dirty potsherds is the proper business of an archaeologist at all. Archaeologists supervise while labourers extract priceless and beautiful objects from tombs. To the man in the street, even the High Street of Peter's home village of Fellingham, in Broadshire, all archaeologists must be professors, and as such, must be elevated both culturally and intellectually, so that they could converse on equal terms with Her Ladyship, at The Manor, and with the Rector, who could read Greek.

Local archaeology depends to a large extent on getting information and objects from people. Of the material collected, it is true, only a small proportion is relevant. The archaeologist must therefore collect and select for himself. Peter went out of his way to be conspicuous. A small, thick-set man, he nevertheless stood out in a crowd because of his bright check shirts, deer-stalkers' hat, and large black beard.

There was absolutely no doubt that Peter was an eccentric. He could talk foundations with the builders, and drains with the navvies. He even found time to listen to old Mrs. Smith's long catalogues of complaints and gossip, which usually included references to changes which had occurred in the village, buildings demolished, roads diverted, or to what had been found at the back of the *Rose and Crown* when they dug the new cesspit fifty years ago. He was often beseiged by small children with things they had dug up in their gardens.

Like the man who makes a better mousetrap than his fellows, Peter, who made a good listener, and an even better talker, and who never mocked any of the strange things which were brought to him, had a path beaten to the front door of his cottage. Not that the path needed beating literally. His front door opened directly from a narrow pavement into the room which acted as living room and study. There were only three other rooms to what had been until recently, a working man's terrace cottage. Peter had a study-cum living room, a modern kitchen, a bedroom and what are euphemistically called 'usual offices' in estate agents' lists. And, of course, a well stocked cellar below. He lived in lonely luxury in these quarters, which, fifty years before, when what was now the bathroom was the second bedroom, and the privvy was in the back yard, had served for a family of seven. Peter felt no guilt for turning the working man from his home; he, or rather his descendants, lived in subsidised luxury in the estate built by the council on the high ground overlooking the village.

The treasures which Peter was called upon to examine covered a wide spectrum, from odd-shaped stones, of

8

natural geological origin, to common objects which have become obsolete quite unremarked by most people. To a ten-year-old child, a milkbottle with a recessed top for a cardboard cover, belongs to the remote past, having had no use in the child's lifetime. Even a metal stopper for a hot water bottle is a mystery, the function of which cannot be guessed.

As quickly as the use of an object is forgotten, so, often, is its origin. He frequently had some quite interesting item brought to him: a Roman coin, or even, once, a mediaeval battleaxe, with the story that it was brought home by old dad, or grandad, who used to be a gardener, but its provenance was forgotten. Peter felt duty bound to treat all comers with patience, and to discuss every item, no matter how trivial it might appear to others, with interested attention. It was important to Peter that he should be somehow different, but not anti-social. As for breaking the law, that would never do. Apart, that is, from such minor transgressions as trespassing on his neighbour's building site when the foundations were being dug, and taking away, without permission, certain objects, to wit, fragments of mediaeval pottery, being the property of the said neighbour.

That was why there was some gossip in the village one morning during the school summer holidays (Peter was a schoolmaster and taught, of all things, chemistry), when the local archaeologist was evidently 'taken in for questioning'. He was standing looking in a shop window 'all innocent like', when a heavy hand fell on his shoulder, and the best blue voice of the local representative of the Broadshire Constabulary, PC 359 Harris, K, was heard by witnesses to say, 'Mr Wood? I wonder if you would mind accompanying me to the Station?'

'And 'e went along as good as gold,' old Mrs Smith reported later to her friends at the Old Folks' Club. 'I wonder what 'e's gone and done?'

9

What the village gossips could not know was the conversation that went on as the policeman escorted his prisoner away.

'The fact is, I've dug something up in my garden that I'd like you to have a look at, sir. Sort of pot. Never seen anything like it myself, though I don't expect it's of much interest to you really. It's got printing on it. Great big capital letters. Must be too modern to be archaeological.'

So Peter entered the Police Station, which was an excrescence on the side of PC Harris's police issue house, occupying the position and space usually reserved for a garage, with not quite the apprehension that the Fellingham ladies imagined. The constable put on the kettle, and produced a large and official-looking manilla envelope. From the envelope he drew a buff-coloured, shallow pottery bowl, with a wide flanged rim, in which there was a pouring lip. The inside of the vessel was covered with sharp grit, fired into the clay. On the rim was stamped DOINV.

Peter explained, as they sipped tea, that the pot was Roman, and was a mortar, used for pulping food. Of *course* the lettering was modern—the finest example of lettering ever done was in Rome, on Trajan's column.

Later they went outside to visit the scene of the crime, and Peter noted the place where the pot had come up with a root of PC Harris's early crop potatoes. The resulting excavation does not need reporting here. It is adequately published already in Volume XXIV of the *Transactions of the Broadshire Archaeological, Antiquarian & Architectural Society*. The only relevance it has to the present story is that it led to a friendship between a policeman and an archaeologist, which lasted when the policeman was promoted away to the regional headquarters. 'Detective Inspector Harris? Oh yes, I know him quite well. I once helped him dig his potatoes.'

Peter Wood was therefore 'known to the police', and became involved, because of his specialist knowledge, in the nasty affair at the Cold Beech Villa. Although he never had any official standing in the investigation, the Inspector managed to take him along. After all, you need an inveterate collector of gossip in a murder enquiry. And the Inspector knew from experience that there is no-one like a field archaeologist to explain unlikely associations of objects.

CHAPTER 2

Death

The affair began, as far as Peter was concerned, on a Sunday morning in early autumn, when the harvest was all in, but the frosts had not yet started. The Broadshire County Council were straightening a stretch of what had been, before the motor-car ceased to be a luxury and became a necessity, a pretty stretch of winding country lane, with high hedges of considerable antiquity. Peter and his friends had done what they could. A quick survey of the lane had been made, with particular reference to making a record of all the perennial plant species in the hedges. It is perhaps not widely realised that this information can be of help in deciding just how long the hedges had been in existence.

A quick look through the gazeteer of known findspots, held by Peter for the local archaeological groups, had shown that nothing of interest had been found in the locality, apart from the usual ubiquitous scattering of flint implements of all prehistoric periods. Nevertheless, a close watch had been kept on the work of the engineers as it had gonᵥ forward. On the Saturday morning, a telephone call from one of the observers on the site had informed Peter that a single pot, clearly a Roman cooking pot, had been turned up and shattered by a machine digging a drainage trench. Inside it had been a mass of small pieces of burnt bone. This was clearly indication of the presence of at least one cremation burial. A series of telephone calls had resulted in his obtaining permission to investigate, and a small but experienced gang of archaeologists to do the work.

Work had begun very early, before the sun had dispersed the thin mist which hung close to the ground. The areas to be excavated had been marked out before the milkman had passed in his electric float, and by the time the earliest of the day trippers had begun to stream past on their way to take advantage of what might be their last day at the seaside, the diggers had already begun to disappear into the landscape. Archaeologists at work in the field are not usually conspicuous, because they conceal themselves in holes in the ground. On this site they tended also to adopt an accidental camouflage. A natural spring which had made the drainage trenches necessary, had waterlogged the top-soil, which was thus turned into a slurry by the contractor's machines; the diggers were plastered with a thin layer of this material before they reached the dryer material below.

Peter Wood was quite immersed in his hobby. If the policeman in the car had not noticed him earlier in the day, he might have stayed immersed. It was a Sunday morning, and all good navvies were at their devotions. Peter was on his knees, but the apparent object of his worship was nothing but a small nest of broken pots, which he was religiously cleaning with a knife and a paintbrush. He looked up at the polite cough from the uniformed figure which looked so out of place standing on the muddy spoil from the trench.

'Excuse me. Are you Mr Peter Wood?'

'That's right. Can I help you?'

'I have just received a message over the car radio to pick you up and take you to Cold Beech Roman Villa. Inspector Harris would like a word with you.'

'Can you get him on that portable set you've got there?'

'I should be able to through headquarters, sir.'

'Just do that for me. Tell him I'm busy, unless it's very urgent.'

The policeman looked slightly surprised.

'Go on.'

'X-Ray 3 to HQ.'

'Come in X-Ray 3.'

'I have a message for Inspector Harris. Over.'

13

'X-Ray 3. Wait.' There was a short silence. 'Harris here—what's wrong, Jones?'

'It's the gentleman you asked me to pick up. He says he's busy, unless it's urgent. Over.'

The officer handed the little walkie-talkie set to Peter who had played with one of these before. He held it close to his face.

'Look here Ken, I've got trouble enough with dead Romans without being chivvied about by coppers. What's eating you? Over.'

He was amused to see the look of amazement on the face of the man sent to fetch him. It said quite clearly 'This grubby little man can only be one of the labourers on this site. If he talks like that to Inspector Harris, he's going to find himself inside without touching the ground.'

The set crackled.

'To Hades with dead Romans! Come here at once. I've got a blasted dead archaeologist over here for you. Over and out.'

The policeman gave Peter a hand out of the trench (and got a muddy hand himself for his pains) and waited while the archaeologist walked over to another trench to give instructions to a grubby figure. He then escorted him back to the car, and held the door for him, obviously wishing that he had been asked to bring back something which would make less of a mess of the upholstery and carpet. In a short time they were speeding down the road in the direction of Cold Beech Villa.

To Peter it was going back over old ground. But going much faster than he used to do it when he was a schoolboy, and rode every day during the holidays along the twisting lanes to 'The Dig' on his bicycle. 'The Dig'—Cold Beech Roman Villa, to give it a more specific title—has in fact ceased to be a dig at all. When work first began on it, it had been a quiet hillside, overgrown with hawthorn scrub. The diggers had been serenaded by a chorus of birds, including

14

nightingales. Wild flowers had bloomed all around. Now the place had changed. The Villa had proved attractive to the Ancient Monuments Department, who had provided it with what was euphemistically called 'a permanent shelter'—a hideous low building in asbestos cement corrugated sheeting, with a corrugated translucent roof. The wild flowers had been treated with selective weedkiller. The grass was trimmed and edged with whitewashed stones. What had been a beautiful spot was now a cross between an army camp and a battery farm.

The car swept into the regimental car park beside the Villa. The peaked-capped attendant in the sentry box looked over the top of his tabloid newspaper, saw that these were not customers, and went back to reading the sports page. Peter got out and marched up to the double doors of the permanent shelter, which were guarded by a helmeted constable. After a brief exchange, he was admitted. The Inspector came over to meet him, leaving a small group of men who appeared to be busy with cameras and tape measures.

'Hello Peter—welcome to my *villa* very *rustica*.'

'What have you got for me, Ken? Tell me all about it.'

'There's not very much to tell yet, but it's obviously a sitter for an archaeologist. This morning at half-past eight, the custodian of this ancient monument, Mr Black, came to work as usual.'

'Bit early, wasn't he? I thought they opened at 9.30?'

'He says there's a lot to do to sort out the sales desk, balance up the books and so on. He likes to swab down the mosaic floor so that it's nice and bright for his first customers—'

'Who are just about due, I should think,' said Peter.

'No culture today, I think. We've put a man on the door, and the car park man can turn the more affluent people away. As I was saying: Mr Black arrived at 8.30, to find the main door and the emergency exit open.'

15

'Open? You mean that? Not unfastened?'

'They were wide open. The double doors were fastened back by the hooks provided by the architects. The emergency exit was held open by a chair taken from the office. Naturally, Mr Black was alarmed, and suspected either vandalism or theft. He checked the office: everything undisturbed, except for the missing chair. He then walked rapidly round the site, looking for signs of damage. Nothing. He'd just decided that it must be some sort of prank, when he found the body.'

'Where was it? And who was it?' said Peter, all agog.

'Remember there is a well beside the villa, but inside this building?'

'Of course I do. *I* excavated it longer ago than I care to recall.'

'There is always a little fresh water in it?' asked the Inspector.

'That's right. Only a couple of feet at the most. Not fresh, though. Something to do with this translucent roof or something like that. The water was always bright green. But you are supposed to be telling me about this body.'

'Down the well. Drowned apparently.'

'Must have fallen down, knocked himself out on the side. You must be unconscious to drown in two feet of water. *Who was it*?' Peter's voice rose almost to a shout, and the men at the far side of the building all looked round.

'Major Frederick Forbes, OM, FSA, etc, the Director of Excavations for the County Archaeological Society. I don't think this one can be an accident, either. There is no evidence on the body of his having fallen—no bruises or anything like that. That suggests he must have climbed down a ladder. But he didn't climb back up it. Someone else took it out of the well and left the old boy down there. It's odd that he didn't try to climb out. Just lay down and drowned. There are other odd features,' the Inspector went on, 'for instance, why had Forbes taken off his shoes, socks, and

16

trousers before going down there to drown? Why did he fill his jacket pockets with several poundsworth of small change to weigh his body down? And why did he take his shrimping net with him? And why on earth was he here at midnight?'

CHAPTER 3

Routine Enquiries

Peter was persuaded to view the body, now removed from the well and lying in a large puddle. He had often dealt with the dead, scatching the earth from between their bones. He had always tried to imagine that the skeletons he was exhuming had been people at one time, with ideas, motives and lives of their own. As he looked at the body of the Major, once so upright and military in his manner, he realised that he was glad that he had never really succeeded in clothing his dead Saxons or Romans with flesh. Modern death was somehow sickening. This was the mere shell of a man, huddled here. He had been tall, ruddy-faced, and impeccably dressed, with neat, short, iron-grey hair, well brushed, and a neat, clipped moustache. Now he was a limp, shrunken heap. His face was almost the same colour as his hair, which was disarrayed and spread out in damp rats' tails. He was unshaven, and the final indignity was that he wore short underpants, but no trousers, shoes or socks. He had a distinct odour of stagnant water.

Peter turned away.

'I don't like this game, my captain!' he said to the Inspector. 'I like my bodies respectably buried for a few hundred years. You go on and do your own thing. Find out all you can. Collect data like a good archaeologist. If there's anything you still need to know by sunset, when I'll have finished down my holes, and you think I can help, come along to the *White Horse* in the village, and we'll solve it over a few jars of ale.'

So, much later that day, when the light was too poor for digging, Peter and Ken were sitting comfortably in a fairly quiet and private corner of the quietest of the local

18

hostelries, each with a pint tankard.

'Right. Fire away. Tell me all you've found out so far.'

'And astonishingly little that seems to be when you boil it down to its essence,' said the Inspector. 'Deceased, as you know, was Major Albert Forbes, OM, FSA, retired with a pension from the Artillery, as far as I can make out. Knocking on seventy, but still amazingly active. Still directed excavations for the County Archaeological Society. Quite a famous old boy, in his own sphere, by all accounts. Despite all this success, it seems difficult to trace any close friends, or even enemies, for that matter. Lived on his own in a little cottage not far from the Villa at which he met his death.

'He attended a meeting of the County Archaeological Society last night. It seems he took part in the discussion after the lecture. Had coffee after the meeting, in the hall with the other members; circulated around, apparently radiating good spirits. Had a long talk with the speaker, a Professor Charleston, and left quite late, probably about eleven. He drove away in his own car, we surmise. At least we know he arrived in it at the hall, and it was in his garage this morning. He died, certainly from drowning, just after midnight. You know how the body was found, and the rather grotesque circumstances. We have had men out checking up on his activities last night, but we've no idea what happened to him after he left the meeting, which was at Broadchester, the county town, about ten miles from the Villa. We don't know what he was doing with no trousers on down the well in the middle of the night, loaded down with money to make him sink, and with a shrimping net as what you digging people would call "grave goods".'

'My, you police people do live sheltered lives, don't you? I can tell you what he was doing. It's the old *Coventina* syndrome at work. But let's get some of the other facts needed for a complete report on the ritual deposit. First question: did you find the ladder?'

'Oh yes we used it to get the body out of the hole. It was a part of the furtniture in the Villa shelter. Light aluminium job, used for cleaning skylights, getting birds' nests out of gutters and so on.'

'It wasn't in the well when the body was found?'

'No—it was lying tidily by the back wall of the building.'

'What was the cause of death?'

'Drowning, as I told you!'

'No,' said the archaeologist, 'water in his lungs was what *killed* him, if your doctor says so. But that didn't cause his death in the sense that I mean. An active man like Forbes doesn't lie down in a couple of feet of water for fun, and forget to get up again. What happened to make him drown? Heart attack, cramp, or what?'

'There's the rub,' said the Inspector. 'I just don't know. The doctor couldn't help either. He says that there were no signs of violence at all, and no signs of disease to account for a collapse. We must postulate foul play anyway. Someone must have taken the ladder away, so whoever it was must have known he was down there.'

'And the time of death is clearly established, without any doubt?'

'As near as we can tell. The doctor seemed quite happy at "somewhere between midnight and two am." The Major's watch had given up trying to work under water at twelve-ten. Now you tell me something. Why *was* he down there in the semi-undress at that time in the morning? What has Covent Garden got to do with it?'

'Not Covent Garden. *Coventina*. Let me get you another pint.' Peter took the tankards over to the bar, as the Inspector sat glaring after him. 'I'll give you another clue. What does *Trevi* mean to you?'

'I didn't come to play word associations with you,' growled Ken, as the full tankards were returned. '*Trevi* is a place, isn't it, in Italy?'

'Rome. Oh come on.'

20

'Ah! Fountains! Not wells, though.'

'What is special about *that* fountain?'

'Got it! Three coins in the fountain and all that!'

'Right you are. Everyone nowadays throws money into wishing wells, or almost any other exposed piece of water. The fountain in the Greek and Roman gallery in the British Museum is always littered with small change. Even the little pond in our local florists. Coventina's Well was up on Hadrian's Wall; it had nearly thirteen and a half thousand coins chucked in it—that was over a long period, and she *was* a goddess. But people have gone on chucking money away ever since.'

'Do you mean to tell me that old Forbes was down there scrabbling for small change?' asked the Inspector, aghast.

'It's inescapable. The shrimping net isn't what the archaeologist would call an "accidental association". You don't often find such things at Roman villas; especially ones so far from the sea. Anyway, he must have gone down there of his own free will. You almost said as much yourself.'

'Blimey! What a turn up for the book!' said the policeman, inelegantly. 'They really caught the old boy with his trousers down, and no mistake.'

'You're really determined that it can't be natural causes then?'

'It might be, I suppose. But we'd still have some joker wandering about who must have known, and didn't tell. Let's treat it as being death in suspicious circumstances, at the very least. What else would you need to know, as a digger, to report on this find?'

'All the associated objects, please, and how they are associated.'

'Apart from all that small change, not a lot. Wallet containing the usual things, driving licence, library ticket and so on, one pound note, cigarette case and lighter in trouser pockets; and a bunch of keys. One of them fitted the door into the Villa, so he came prepared.'

'Is that all?' asked the archaeologist.

The Inspector looked in a pocket book. 'That's all.'

'Notice anything missing?'

'Not especially. Help a poor bobby out.'

'How did you see the body when you got there?'

'Sun shining through the translucent roofing. We could have put the flourescent lights on if it had been a dull day,' said the Inspector.

'If you'd been there at two in the morning, and you'd put the lights on, someone would have been sure to have noticed. You can see the site for miles. You'll have to check that one. I would have expected a torch on the body.'

'My turn to buy a round,' said the policeman, rising to his feet. 'I wouldn't think that the old boy would have advertised his presence by putting the light on. You've got something there.'

When the full tankards returned, Peter had his diary open.

'There was a full moon last night. He must have worked by moonlight.'

'Blast! What do we do now? I suppose we check up on the torch and try to find out if anyone did see lights at the Villa last night, but I expect you're right.'

'How much small change had the Major collected before he met his maker?'

Out came the notebook again.

'Four pounds nineteen and a penny, two francs and three pfennigs,' the Inspector read out. 'Quite a load when you imagine it was all in coppers.'

'Tomorrow I think we should check up on Forbes' banking habits. He must have done it before. At least we can try to find out whether *his* crime was premeditated. That might tell us something about the other crime—if it was a crime.'

'What else should we do?' asked the Inspector.

'I like the royal "we",' said Peter. 'I think "we" will go and meet the last people to see the Major alive. Before that, you will have to undergo a quick familiarisation course on recognising classes of archaeologists. If you can recognise their field marks and habits, and know their various biases, it may help to find out from them what did happen last night. Leave the routine enquiries and all that sordid business to the other ranks. You must go gossiping with the county archaeologists. You mustn't believe a word they say, of course. I'll explain.'

He rose, and went to have the tankards refilled.

CHAPTER 4

Them and us

Peter made himself comfortable, and began in his best tutorial manner.

'The field archaeologist is like a detective. The essential difference between us, usually, is that the first thing *you* know is what crime was performed, and the information you intend to deduce is who dunnit. The archaeologist, on the other hand doesn't even know, at the outset, what was done, let alone who was responsible. In fact, the last thing that an excavator would expect to be able to deduce would be the identity of a specific person. Our job, at best, is to blame some specific group for the phenomena that we discover. Often we deliberately beg the question, and name the group from the evidence that we have observed. For example, one archaeologist described the material he had discovered as being proof of the activities of a group of "equestrian inhumators", because they rode horses, and buried their dead. Another, more humanistic, archaeologist pointed out that on evidence collected at Perry Bar, he concluded that the inhabitants of Birmingham were a race of "tram-riding cremators". At the outset, I suppose we might provisionally describe the man we are looking for as belonging to a well-sacrificing group. We might, as a start, then try to find out more about the group to which this person belongs, before we try to locate the individual member of that group.

'The first thing that must be remembered in any discussion of any group of people,' he went on, 'is that the group consists of individuals. In fact, not to put too fine a point on it, of both individuals and individualists—followers and leaders. In archaeology there is rivalry between individuals, and there is rivalry between the societies which exist around the individuals. It is this continual feeling of "us and them" which makes it so difficult to actually achieve anything in archaeology. If all the archaeologists agreed on what needed doing, and all did it together, it is difficult to imagine what they might not do.

'Just to simplify matters,' said Peter, as the Inspector glared reproachfully at him over his pint, 'let us divide the whole of Gaul into four parts. Let us call them: Academic, County, Dirt and Museum. These are the main divisions into which the archaeologists can be arbitrarily put. It is between these that the main political frictions occur. Not that there's not a lot of in-fighting within each faction. It is the rivalry between individuals which leads to homicide. Obviously it was *a person* that did for old Forbes, not a faction. But it will help us if we can put him into his right phylum as it were.'

'Not so much as it would help us if we could find his fingerprints on some weapon,' growled Ken Harris, as he took the tankards to the bar to be refilled. 'Go on with the lesson in taxonomy. You were dividing your lot into four warring factions I think!' he went on as he returned.

'Not *my* lot please,' said Peter, 'I'm an individualist. Anyway, I must try to stand aloof, and practice scientific detachment, if you are to get anything like an unbiased picture.'

'Unbiased fiddlesticks! You're the most jaundiced observer of human behaviour I've ever met; and I've never believed anything you tell me since that business with the five-legged stool.'

Peter grinned wryly and sipped his beer. He had never been forgiven by either his friends or his enemies for a spoof article he wrote for the Proceedings of the Prehistoric Society. Inspired by a serious paper on interpretation of post holes found in the subsoil under prehistoric sites—were they watchtowers, granaries, stores, houses, or 'above-ground burials' of all things—he had invented a mythical

25

excavation where the holes were in groups of five, and written the whole thing from his head, with numerous explanations backed by historical and ethnographical parallels, with bibliography. It had been printed before someone thought to check one of the references, and found that it was an invention.

'Don't bring that up, or I won't play,' he said without rancour. 'I'll tell you what I'll do. I'll give you the blackest picture of each faction that I can think of. You can imagine each of the factions seeing the others as I have painted them. When you go around collecting statements, I'll chip in quietly and classify the person you have interviewed for you, so that you know what his bias is. But don't forget, anything anyone says about another individual may be biased because he hates his guts, or because he admires him, or because he is overcompensating for hating him.'

'Thanks for nothing,' said the Inspector. 'I don't expect archaeologists are really much worse than the rest of humanity.'

'Don't you believe it. They murder one another's reputations every day at breakfast without turning a hair. It does surprise me to find extreme physical violence, though I do remember a time on the dig down at Dun—'

'Back to the point, please!'

'Right! What did I say? Academic, County, Museum and Dirt. Sounds like the divisions of the Guards: Fire, life, mud, and black. First victims for verbal assassination: the Academics. Curious birds, living in ivory towers far from the madding throng. Chief occupation seems to be reorganising what other people have done. You know the sort of thing: to quote from one source without acknowledgement is plagiarism, but to quote from many with a page of references is research. Occasionally emerge from their colleges to do some set-piece excavation, preferably under ideal conditions, but with completely untrained students to do the work. Result is immaculate

26

confusion. Site looks marvellous, but the interpretation of the two week excavation keeps the academic director busy for the rest of the year, and his fellow academics will still be discussing his work for the next twenty years. The biggest crimes in archaeology as far as they can see would be: a site that looks untidy in the photographs, plagiarism, a clear and lucid account of one's work, and having missed a recent reference which might have some marginal application to the report or paper in hand.'

'Or being found out, I suppose,' put in the Inspector.

'Yes, but they wouldn't actually kill one another for bad academic discipline. The rapier of invective in some erudite journal might suit the case: "I note that in *Antiquity*, volume xiiii part 2 page seven-hundred and thrumpty that Professor Blob refers to the St Pancras and Mornington Crescent People. Surely he is aware that Bungler, in *Zeitschrift fur Angst und Drang*, Bild 7 nummer 2 has demolished the theory that there is any connection between St Pancras and Mornington Crescent, and demonstrated that the two sites should be considered separately. In any case the term 'people' used in this context (Bungler *volk*) should be replaced by the more up-to-date expression cultural-sub-assemblage put foward by Libby in *Archaeobiometrica* ... etc etc"—you know the sort of thing.'

'I do indeed. What happens to the poor Professor Blob?'

'Usually this sort of thing is so trivial anyway that no-one but the editor and writer even bother to read it. To continue. Verbal assassination No.2: The County. County archaeological societies were formed in the first half of the nineteenth century if they are to be of any standing at all. They are placed in a pecking order which depends entirely on age. Not of the members, but of the Society. The Broadshire Society, BAAAS, is much superior to the Weffolk Field Club. The former was founded in 1846, and the latter in 1848. To look at them you would get the impression that some of the founders still attend general meetings. Originally the idea of being an antiquary began as a cultural thing; like keeping useless deer in your park rather than useful sheep, it demonstrated to the world that you had the leisure to do something unproductive. The idea still lingers on. It's too good for the common people. I expect they'd do the same for sex if they could. To be a member of the County Society you must be upper middle class or above. The President is a lady (a real one) with a degree in history. The leading lights were for years the clergy. To direct a successful excavation one must be a retired army officer.'

'They'll be electing a new Director next meeting! I wonder if that's a motive?'

'Doesn't seem likely; it's not a paid post like secretary, though there may be perks, like the kudos, and the possibility of lecturing to Women's Institutes for meagre fees—'

'Which is all right if you're a masochist. Continue.'

'The major crime against the County Set would be not belonging to it. They cannot abide archaeologists who dare to set shovel to dirt without the Queen's commission or the benefit of clergy. They usually suffer the museum people, at curator level, and the academic people, at professor level, as being on a par in the great chain of being.'

'It sounds as though they would use a horsewhip to a transgressor, rather than a more lethal weapon. I wonder what the weapon was, by the way. Anyway, the Major was one of them.'

'Certainly not one of *us*. Third candidate for the block: the Dirt archaeologists. A product of modern education, firm believers in the old saying "what one fool can do, another one can do better", a race of diggers not blessed by academic qualification, army commission, or theological disputation. Many of them are good technicians, although they all criticise one another unmercifully. Most of them are competent to do the job of excavating, but are beyond the pale because they have no cultural polish. They even look upon the academic discussions with ridicule. In fact the others would say that they ought not to be allowed, because they can't possibly understand the implications of their digging. Most of them are a bit bolshy too. They look upon the past as being part of everybody's heritage. They are the ones you will find saving potsherds from under bulldozers. A thankless and dangerous task. The prof at one of the Midland universities recently said that he thought that no excavation at all was better than a hurried and un-planned one, where the results might be misleading. He was the man who was doing his seventeenth season on a minor Roman villa in a secluded deerpark while a motorway destroyed half a Roman town on his doorstep.'

'You're getting partisan!' put in the Inspector. 'Cool down and have another pint.'

'Sorry. The chief crime to a dirt archaeologist is to squander manpower and money. Destruction of sites should be anticipated. Publication should be cheap and lucid. They suffer the academics because someone has to discuss the background of mere digging. You never find anyone trained at a university wasting his time digging this way.'

'What would they want to do in old Forbes for?'

'Nothing premeditated. I could imagine one of them pushing the old boy under a bulldozer if he came and pontificated on their rescue excavation. I could imagine him taking a pot shot at one or two of them, however.'

'You've got to the Museums.'

'Last, and probably least, the Museums. They tend to affiliate themselves to the County and the Academic. In origin they come from the efforts of the County brigade in the old days at robbing barrows and bringing home other peoples' cultural heritage from the Grand Tour. Nowadays they all have degrees, so feel they are bringing truth to the ignorant. Most of them also have qualifications which can

29

only be obtained by people working in museums—the sort of mystique which exists in many professional closed shops. Remember the fuss there was over the idea of charging for admission to museums? The curators were against charging on the grounds that education should be free. The cynical saw this in a different light. They wondered what would happen to the museums if they had to make a profit. The museums in this county cannot be said to run for the benefit of the public. They both open at ten and close at four, shut for an hour at lunch time and all afternoon on early closing days, and don't open on Sundays. The only time the Curator, assistant curator, secretary, and three custodians see any customers is on wet days in the school holidays.'

'Sounds as though they are good candidates for homicide, but not very likely murderers. What are the motives for their becoming violent?'

'I'm sure they are all quite harmless. And very likeable people too. Apart from the impression they try to give of perpetual motion without anything changing, they seem quite ineffectual. They might get a bit worked up if a nice juicy exhibit were to go to a rival museum; but they'd probably breathe a sigh of relief that they wouldn't have the job of preserving or exhibiting it.'

'Time gentlemen please!' said the landlord, removing Inspector Harris's tankard before he had emptied it. 'Come along now, gents all. We don't want the police in here, do we?'

CHAPTER 5

Meeting the county

When Peter woke next morning, refreshed by a night's sleep made deeper by strong ale, he had a feeling of suppressed excitement. He was still on holiday; summer was gracefully turning into autumn; there was a problem awaiting solution. A problem rather like the ones so often met with in his hobby. A problem dependent upon the answering of a number of subsidiary questions. A 'deposit' had been discovered, and recorded. The question most necessary to be answered, in this case was: who had made the deposit? In other words, who had been responsible for, or at least the conscious agent in, the deposition of the mortal remains of the late Major F Forbes? This was the essential question as far as the rest of society was concerned. The classical detective approach was to look for three coincidental factors in one person: motive, means and opportunity. If the motive was one of the ordinary, run-of-the-mill ones, like personal gain, then the police procedure, like the mills of God, would grind inexorably until a solution was found, and the murderer was inevitably revealed. Perhaps it was wishful thinking to hope that the motive, like the crime, might be sufficiently out of the ordinary to provide him with food for thought.

He thought all this as he consumed a large breakfast. The inner man being satisfied, he lit his pipe and debated with himself what he should do. How best could he involve himself in what was undoubtedly none of his business? The question was answered for him by a heavy knocking on the front door. On the step stood Detective Inspector Harris. His lean face held an expession which Peter felt sure would make any hardened criminal wish that he had fled through the back door, rather than answered the front one. His steel grey eyes belied the rest of his features.

'Ready?' he asked.

'Ready for what?' Peter asked, obtusely.

'You did say *we* would have to go and chat with the County archaeologists, didn't you? Come on, you should get up earlier. It's a lovely day for a drive.' The Inspector turned on his heel, and went back to his car.

Peter put on a pair of walking shoes, and hurried out to the car. As he got in, Ken Harris started off down the road.

'Where are we going?' Peter asked, as he struggled with the safety belt.

'We must begin with the County set, I think. Last place Forbes was seen alive was at one of their meetings. One of the first things to do is to try to reconstruct his last hours.'

'Do you usually start an enquiry with finding the opportunity, then? Surely there's a lot of more mundane and vital things to be done. What about the enquiries on the spot; what about the motives, finding out who will benefit and all that?'

'We don't need to bother the Director, or even the site supervisors, with stripping the turf and removing the topsoil. We, that is the 'tec in charge and his acting sergeant (you), perform the functions of director and supervisor on this site. We make sure the overall plan is kept up correctly, and decide how the work shall be allocated. We keep an eye on the finds, and if we are lucky, do a bit of the finer trowelling. We co-ordinate the work. In other words, let a few big-footed coppers go around gathering the routine information.'

'Are we going trowelling then?'

'That's it. A bit of the finer work, calling for expert knowledge. This morning we go to see the Secretary of the Broadshire Society—'

'You mean the Broadshire Archaeological, Antiquarian and Architectural Society. *The* Broadshire Society are a different lot altogether. Conservation and all that,' Peter butted in.

'A rose by any other name. What can I call it that doesn't take so long to say that listeners are bored to death?'

'Some say "Bee-ay-ay-ay-ess", others say "Broadshire Arch Soc".'

'We are going to see the Secretary of what you said. A Dr Broad, lives out at Codsden, in a farmhouse,' the Inspector said, through clenched teeth.

'Bloody old Bill Broad! We're going to have fun. Are you hoping to find something out?' said Peter, irreverently.

'And why not, pray? The last place Forbes was seen alive, as far as we know, was at a meeting of the—'

'Broadshire Archaeological, Antiquarian and Architectural Society.'

'How right you are. The obvious person to tell us what happened at that meeting is the Secretary of the Society.'

'You've got a hope. In my experience, the last person to ask for information about *any* county archaeological society is its secretary. He performs an entirely different function. There are outings secretaries, and meetings secretaries to deal with the work. *The* secretary keeps the minutes, which are always taken as read, and preserves the intact respectable facade of the Society. I'm afraid they only converse with their peers,' said Peter.

'You *are* a ruddy cynic,' growled Harris. 'I'll bet you a quick pint at lunchtime that we are told with no difficulty at all everything we want to know about that meeting straight away.'

By this time the car was winding through typical Broadshire sunken lanes with high hedges. Perhaps, Peter Wood thought, typical was not quite the right word. Perhaps the word vestigial was almost applicable. Any road that led anywhere had been straightened. Many hedges had been uprooted to make prairies for the combine farmers, and what trees remained were prematurely yellowed by the scorched earth policy which seemed to go with combine

33

harvesting. He was pleased to see that this set of lanes evidently didn't lead anywhere. He had a vague recollection of Codsdenbury Farm, where Dr Broad lived. A charming old timber-framed building, amongst a cluster of elms, containing the local rookery.

'Tell me about this man Broad, so I know how to tackle him,' said the Inspector.

'I've never met him. We have corresponded, or rather I have written to him a number of times. Never had an answer, now I come to think of it. I suppose I asked the wrong sort of questions. Used to be a rather high-powered doctor in the County town. Became MOH—Officer of Health, not Master of Hounds. Must have been a man of substance in his own right. Married or inherited money. Retired early. Writes notes on heraldic devices for the BAAAS transactions. I always imagine he has the Great Seal of the Society locked away in a hermetically sealed safe to stop the members from breathing on it. That sort of person. Cor! Blindoldriley!'

This last inelegant remark was occasioned by their turning into the drive of Codsdenbury Farm. Gone was the rookery. There were no trees now in the square acre except three standard roses. Square was a description of the garden, not a tautological description of the area. Surrounded by a fence made of white painted boards horizontally attached to white pointed posts, four square, was a perfectly plain green lawn, quite smooth up to the house. Through the lawn sprouted three white lamposts, which might have been more at home on a Victorian railway station. The house itself, which once fitted into the landscape as if it had grown there, was transformed. Gone were the small windows of yesteryear, replaced by large picture windows. The timber framing was now 'a feature' of the architecture. Painted black, it provided a perfect framing for the infilling, now rendered quite flat, and painted a bright turquoise. The Doctor had added a timber-framed

34

garage, for two cars. The drive ended in an area of sterile gravel about the size of two tennis courts. The Inspector parked his rather battered official car next to the Doctor's Jaguar XK 140.

'I think we'd better sterilise our boots to avoid contamination of his carpets,' muttered the archaeologist as they waited for the door to be opened.

The door was opened by Dr Broad himself. A large, pink man, exuding confidence. The sort of person, Peter thought, who could take your appendix out when you were admitted for a broken leg, and feel absolutely certain that it was all for the best because it would save trouble later on. His tweed suit, obviously cut for the countryman image that the wearer wished to project, looked as out of place in the landscape as did the Victorian lamposts.

The Inspector introduced himself, and tactfully avoided a proper introduction of Peter Wood, apart from waving in his direction and saying 'This is my colleague.'

'I was expecting you. Do come in—ah Inspector,' said the Doctor in a mellow, well-modulated, and consciously enunciated voice. 'Would you like a little refreshment after your journey?'

'Thank you sir. What a fine situation you have here,' said Harris, to bridge the social gap as they were ushered into a booklined room. Peter found himself wondering whether the Doctor had bought the books at so much a yard, for their fine bindings, and itched to examine them closely, to read their titles.

'Yes, I think it's a lovely old house,' said the Doctor, in answer to the Inspector's polite, and ironic, observation. 'I think it is important that these—ah—vernacular—ah—buildings—should continue to be used as their builders intended, for comfortable living. I've had a few improvements made, as you no doubt observe.'

While the Doctor attended to some mystery in a section of the bookcase which opened, revealing the books to be

35

false, Peter made excruciated faces at Ken, restoring his face to a polite blankness as the Doctor turned round and handed them the 'little refreshment' he had offered: half pint tankards. Peter accepted his with thanks, raised his glass in salute, and took a strong pull at it. It was full of cream sherry.

'How can I help you, Inspector?' asked the Doctor as they stood rather uncomfortably, holding their tankards.

'I should like to know details of the meeting of the—BAAAS which was held on Saturday,' said the Inspector, looking vainly for somewhere to put down his drink, so that he could get out his notebook. There was no fireplace, so no mantlepiece, and no table. The drink dispensary was closed. He sat down, uninvited, in one of the two leather upholstered chairs, and put his drink down on the white carpeted floor.

'Oh but I've already told you all about that. Over the 'phone. Yesterday.'

'Not quite all about it, sir. I'm afraid we must know who was present, if we are to go ahead with our enquiries,' the Inspector pointed out stolidly.

'I'm sorry, Inspector. I'm sure you must realise that the meetings of an august society such as the Broadshire Archaeological, Antiquarian and Architectural Society are not public meetings, nor is it, so to speak, a public society. One must be proposed by two existing members, and elected by a general meeting. What happens at meetings, apart from what is minuted to appear in our transactions, is therefore, so to speak ah, privileged. I could not divulge information without the instructions of the Council. Our next meeting is in six weeks' time.'

The policeman thought for a moment. Peter thought that he was concealing his irritation perfectly.

'I wonder if I might have the names of the Council members, for a minute, sir?'

'Certainly, Inspector.'

36

A further portion of the bookcase revealed itself to be a bureau desk. From it the Doctor extracted a sheet of paper which he handed to the policeman.

'I see that your Vice-President is Lt Col Sir Willoughby Cresset, the Lord Lieutenant of the County. I wonder if I might speak to him on your telephone?'

'Of course.'

The Doctor led the Inspector to another room, while Peter took the opportunity to look at the covers of the books on the shelf nearest to him. He wondered whether the Doctor really had a taste for early Victorian sermons.

Ten minutes passed. The Doctor and the policeman returned. The former seemed a little downcast, and the latter triumphant.

'All right, officer,' said the Doctor, somewhat ungraciously. 'What would you like to know?'

CHAPTER 6

Proceedings of BAAAS

'What we really want to do,' said Inspector Harris, seating himself in the leather armchair again, 'is to investigate the background of the strange death of Major Forbes. As you know, he was found dead in rather curious circumstances the morning after the last meeting of—er—the Society. Naturally, since we cannot be sure of the cause of death, and we have reason to believe that he may not have been alone when he died, we must investigate the matter in order to satisfy the Coroner's Jury.'

'In what way can I help you then?' asked the Doctor, lighting a cigar.

'You were at the meeting on Saturday. You may have noticed some occurrence which may not have seemed significant at the time, but which might become significant in the context of our enquiry. Perhaps another person present may have noticed something; you can, I hope, tell us who was present at the meeting.'

'Luckily we always sign the book when we go to a meeting, and sign in any visitors whom we might introduce. I can show you the book, and provide you with a list of members. I'm sure that would be highly irregular, but under the circumstances, and if you are prepared to use the list with discretion . . .'

'Of course, Dr Broad. Our investigation is, at the moment, of a sort where publicity is not to be sought, and where willing co-operation by responsible people like yourself is greatly to be valued.'

Dr Broad could be seen to change before their eyes, from obsequiousness, through annoyance to mollified self-satisfaction as the Inspector shamelessly made this libation of soft soap. He rummaged in the bookcase bureau, and emerged with a leather-bound visitors' book, tooled in gold, which he handed to the Inspector.

'Perhaps you would permit me to borrow this. Only for a couple of hours, so that I may have it copied.'

The Doctor looked doubtful.

'I am prepared to sign a receipt for it,' added the Inspector.

'I'm sure that won't be necessary; perhaps you can get it back to me this afternoon?'

'Of course. Perhaps now you could tell us something about the meeting?'

'What sort of thing do you want to know, Inspector?'

'I wish I could answer that. I'm sure you will appreciate that in any enquiry the significant facts are not always apparent. That is why it is so valuable having a discerning observer such as yourself present at this occasion,' said the policeman shamelessly.

The Doctor lapped it up; he thrived on flattery. Sycophancy is often the main motive behind many of the people in office on learned committees, thought Peter to himself. He took a long sip at his sherry, and began to expand.

'It was quite an ordinary meeting really. The speaker was Professor Charleston of Hinkeaton University. He holds the chair of Roman Studies there, you know. Well, his paper was called "Some aspects of Roman Occupation in Broadshire", a very able piece of work which will appear shortly in our transactions.

'After the paper had been delivered, there were some questions from the floor, and a little discussion of one or two points in relation to recent research in the field. Then we had coffee, and went our various ways.'

'What time did the meeting begin, please, Doctor?'

'It began at eight. The business—taking the minutes as read and announcing future activities—took perhaps five minutes. The paper took about an hour and a half. It was illustrated by slides. Questions and discussion brought us to about ten o'clock. Then we had coffee. I imagine we were all out of the hall by eleven at the latest.'

'What time did Major Forbes leave?'

'I can't say I noticed. He was certainly there, circulating among the members. I noticed he was in unusually high spirits for him. He seemed to be elated by something. As if he had made some great discovery, I would say.'

'Was this the result of something that happened at the meeting? I believe he was involved in the discussion after the paper,' put in the Inspector.

'I think it may well be that, Inspector. Yes, he definitely became excited during the discussion.'

'Can you remember what detail was being discussed at the time?' asked Peter. This was clearly entering his domain now.

'Not really. You must remember that I am not a Romanist, but a student of heraldry. It was something about the relationship between a particular site and Roman roads. I'm afraid you'll have to ask someone else for the details.'

Inspector Harris took up the questioning again.

'Can you tell us anything about the deceas—that is, the Major? Personal things,' he added quickly, 'what sort of person he was, and so on.'

'I suppose you know the descriptive stuff: he was a rather typical straightforward military type. No complications, as far as I am aware. Very good director of excavations. Everything according to the drill book.'

'Did he have any friends, in particular, or for that matter, enemies?'

'It's funny, now you come to ask that. I wouldn't know. He certainly went around at meetings talking to people. I can't recollect his ever being associated with any other member, though. He never seemed to arrive with anyone in particular—or leave with anyone, to my knowledge. He

40

always sat by himself at meetings. I noticed that.'

'Did *you* like him, Doctor?'

'I can't honestly answer that one,' said the Doctor after a pause for thought. 'I never really knew him that well. Funny, I'd never thought of that.'

The Inspector rose, and thanked the Doctor for his help.

'Have you a membership list, so that I can find the addresses of the people at the meeting last night, please?'

'I've already put one in the members' signing-in book for you.'

After further thanks on the doorstep, the archaeologist and the policeman escaped again into the mellow Broadshire countryside.

'I thought we were going to have a stiffer time there at first, Ken,' said the archaeologist. 'What on earth did you do to persuade him to help?'

'Phoned the Lord Lieutenant of the County, and explained the situation. I know the old boy quite well from my duties at quarter sessions. He then phoned the President of the Antiques, who phoned Broad and presumably told him not to be such an ass. We've made a start.'

'We haven't got much to go on, though. Let's have a look at that book and see what sort of meeting it was.'

He looked at it a while as the Inspector concentrated on driving along the winding lanes.

'It seems that they had a very successful meeting. At least two people more at it than a normal one. Sixteen souls, including the noble doctor and the Lord Lieutenant. At least we won't have to spend very long on interviews.'

'Thank God for that. I thought these county societies were the power in the land.'

'Quite right. Latent or dormant. Like an iceberg. All sleeping peacefully down below. Lots of money. No action.'

The Inspector turned onto a main road, in the direction of the County Town.

'Time for an early lunch when we've turned this book in

41

for a quick copy. We'd better copy a few pages back as well, in case a pattern emerges, I suppose—who arrives with whom, so to speak. After lunch, we'll go and visit one of the people on the list in it. Who do you suggest?'

'I see that Bill Denny was there as a visitor. He probably didn't do it, but he's one of us—a dirt archaeologist. A good observer. Might give us a lead.'

CHAPTER 7

Down to earth

'You'll find Bill Denny a bit uncouth after old soapy Broad,' observed Peter Wood, as the Inspector threaded his way through the traffic on the outskirts of Broadchester. 'He's not what the County set, or anyone else, would call "cultured". In fact, he's a bit down to earth for even a dirt archaeologist. Still, he's a damn good excavator of the crash-bang-wallop school, and a very shrewd observer—of stratification and life. I'd much rather have *him* behind me than old Doctor Broad. Especially if I was bending down at the time,' he added as an afterthought.

'Don't be crude!' admonished the Inspector. 'Which way do we go now?'

'Turn right under the railway bridge, and straight on.'

The area they were now entering was a dreadful contrast to the 'farmhouse' they had visited in the morning. It was one of those areas where everything seemed to have been forgotten unless it had a function in commerce or motoring. The few houses had a grimy, unwashed, unpainted look. The shops were mostly depressed-looking, as if they had given up any pretence of persuasion. The goods in the windows were pushed in higgledy-piggledy, take it or leave it. The only exception to the dull grime lay in the occasional supermarkets, which stood out as the new temples to Mammon, stark, functional, and clean, with their enormous windows, however, rendered useless by hideous random fluorescent posters screaming loss leaders. Peter indicated a small gateway in a high brick wall, and Harris turned in through it.

Inside the yard was a row of dilapidated sheds. Harris thought to himself that he had never seen the term 'lean-to' so aptly illustrated, and hoped that they wouldn't lean too far while he was in one of them. He parked the car, and as they walked down the length of the muddy yard, sprinkled with brickbats, he tried to glance into one of the sheds to see what went on inside. It was a vain effort, as the windows were thickly covered by cobwebs loaded, apparently, with fine sawdust. As they got nearer to the end of the yard furthest from the road, the Inspector realised that the mud underfoot was now almost entirely composed of sawdust. He looked into one of the sheds through an open door. It seemed to be stacked from floor to roof with assorted and randomly placed offcuts of timber. The next hut was clearly an office. Peter walked up to the door and put his hand on the knob.

'Let me do the talking this time,' he said, and opened the door. As Harris entered, he read the dull anodised aluminium plate which said: 'Wm Denny—Cabinet Maker, French Polisher, Upholsterer. Regd Office.'

The inside of the office was, at first impression, dark; it was also filled with smoke. A large figure rose from a workbench at which he had been sitting, working, as far as Harris could see, under a bright Anglepoise sort of lamp. The figure rather blocked the view. He was an enormous Billy Bunter of a man, wearing metal framed glasses, and smoking a large pipe shaped rather like a well-known make of chemical closet, even to the lid. The Inspector wondered whether this last feature was a normal fitting to this style of pipe, which was probably Germanic in origin, or whether it had been added at the insistence of the insurance brokers who had dared to take on the risk of Denny's premises. The cabinet maker came towards them, moving with that careful light tread which seems a characteristic of heavy men, as though he was afraid he might step through the floor at any moment. When he spoke, it was with a high, almost squeaky voice.

'Hello Uncle Peter. Got a nice juicy demolition and

rebuilding site for me today? One of those lovely "no-time-for-archaeology-it-holds-up-the-work-and-we've-got-a-hefty-penalty-clause-go-away" agents for me to lean on then? And who's your new boy friend?'

Peter introduced Inspector Harris as 'that policeman with the bloody great mortarium in his potato patch, you remember Bill.'

This was evidently the right sort of introduction. Bill opened the window at his side, nearly knocking over a number of potted plants, and yelled, 'Put the kettle on, Ma!' He then removed cardboard boxes from the other two chairs in the room so that they could sit down. While this was going on, Harris glanced over at the workbench with the bright light to see what sort of work this cabinet maker and French polisher could do. He was rather surprised to find that the bright light was an illuminated magnifying glass on an arm which enabled it to be held over, not a cabinet, but a coffin, and not a wooden coffin either. Inside a somewhat distorted leaden casket there was evidently still a body, embedded in plaster or lime. On top of the white material Bill had put down the tools he had been using, which were a scalpel, mounted needle and tweezers.

'Just operating on old Balbus,' he observed, when he saw Harris's obvious interest. 'Someone's got to do it, and that twit in the Museum's about as much use as a pickpocket in a nudist colony.'

He turned to Peter. 'What's up old son, have they found out about you bigamous marriage, or is it that little matter of the illicit still in the school chemistry lab?'

'We have come to see you,' said Peter, ignoring this banter, 'because we want to know something.'

'Not at all, don't mention it. No-one ever comes to see me unless they want something. Fire away, old son.'

'Have you heard about Major Forbes' death?'

'I gather that old fierce-and-friendly went and tumbled down the well. Don't tell me you went and gave the old sod

45

a shove?'

'We don't really know what happened yet,' explained Peter. 'Let's say that "the police are not satisfied that foul play can be ruled out". That sounds the right formula.'

'It's no use coming to me. I never done it, hofficer, honest I never,' Bill wailed as he rolled his eyes piteously. Then he suddenly returned to sanity. 'What time and what day?' he asked sharply.

'As near as we can tell, just after midnight on the morning of Sunday last,' Harris answered.

'Funny,' squeaked Bill Denny, 'I saw him on Saturday night at the Arch Soc meeting. He tried to persuade me that I owed him some money for some offprints of their ruddy transactions. "Not on your Nellie, Fierce Freddy", says I. "Go and fish in some other stream".'

'It looks as if he did—' began Peter, but Harris signalled him to silence.

'It seems that the people at that meeting were the last people to see Forbes alive, apart, perhaps, from the murderer, if there was one,' said the Inspector. 'Can you tell us anything about the meeting that you can remember? It doesn't matter if it seems irrelevant. We really don't know what we're looking for yet, so we're just collecting data.'

'That sounds like a textbook excavation to me. Lots of shiney notebooks full of bumf and numbers; select the bits you want and ditch the rest. Aha!'

This latter expletive was for the appearance of Ma, with the tea.

'Meet the missus,' said Bill, informally waving a hand in her direction. 'Thanks for the extra cups, love.'

'Impressions of the meeting,' prompted Peter, when his cup was full.

'I arrived late, trying to miss all that dreadful "shall-we-take-the-minutes-as-dead-show-of-ancient-hands" procedure. Signed in by old Taff from the Museum I was. He's one of them,' he added darkly. 'The speaker was

46

Charleston, the subject was Roman Broadshire. Like most of these academics he hadn't much to add. Pure cribbing from end to end. Grubby slides. Chunks of rolling Latin to impress the old dears with his erudition. Most of the stuff was rehashed from books, except that about his own dig at Water End. That was the dig he did last year. His slides were very off it too, you know, no scale in them, and poor colour. Almost as if he'd used copies of slides taken by visitors. He could have done better than that.

'After the paper, there were the usual rather obvious sort of questions. Most of the poor old antiques are pretty ignorant anyway. Fierce Freddy asked a question about the Antonine Itinerary, which got rather a dusty answer, I remember.'

'How did Forbes strike you, at that time?' asked Harris.

'A bit more pompous than usual, as if he had some great truth revealed to him alone. He couldn't just ask a question. None of these antiquary Johnnies ever can; they have to make a sort of political speech every time.'

Denny's mobile features underwent a subtle change, and seemed to stiffen and even to thin. His back went straight, and his voice changed. Harris realised that he was watching a natural mimic at play, and that this was the nearest he would ever get to hearing the Major speak.

'I consider that the—aah—the aah speakah tonight is to be aaah congratulated upon aaah a most aaaah excellent and aaaaaah learned aaaah dissertation. I aaaah wondah if he would be so kind as to aaaaha amplify the aaaaaah points that he made . . .'

'Can you remember what the point was that he was aaaah—seeking—aah—to amplify?' said Peter, catching the mannerisms.

'Some stupid idea about Charleston's dig and the ruddy Antonine Itinerary part thrumpty-noo. Couldn't think what the old basket was twittering about really. You can't expect to squeeze much more from that old lemon.'

47

'You say you spoke to Forbes after the meeting?' asked the Inspector.

'During coffee. He was pussyfooting around smarming people. Tried to smarm me out of a couple of quid. Luckily I had his receipt in my wallet. Mean old—'

'*Nil nisi bonum*,' put in Peter.

'Righto! He was a mean old basket when he was alive though!'

'What time did Forbes leave the hall?' asked the Inspector.

'He was one of the last to go. When I left, with Taffy the Museum, he had just sidled up to the speaker and driven him into a corner. I wondered whether the Treasurer had just given the Prof his train fare, and old Fiercesome Fred was trying to cadge if off him.'

'Thanks for your help,' said the Inspector.

'We'll call again if we want something,' said Peter, rising to go.

'You do that,' said Bill. 'I must get on with doing for old Balbus here. His shroud's quite complete inside all this crap. Quite a job, this one. A bit different from the old pick-and-shovel-down-to-the-gravel stuff at the weekend.' They turned to go. 'See you tonight at the Museum. You must come. Old Taffy's going to get on his hind legs and talk about his little scratch at that great big defenceless Neolithic camp of his.'

The archaeologist and the detective retraced their path through the yard to the car in silence.

'I must go back to the office and appear to be doing some work for a change. I'll drop you off at your place on the way,' said Ken.

As they made their slow way through the thickening traffic, they attempted to recap what they had discovered about the last movements of Major Forbes.

'We might as well admit that the routine enquiry going on will probably uncover motive and opportunity that *we'll* get nowhere near. Then I'll get a boot up my backside for wasting my time and the tax-payers' money on gossip. Still, let's see what we've got so far from our side of the enquiries, the archaeological side,' said Ken Harris.

'Yes, you're probably right. We concentrate on the meeting the old boy went to, when all the time the vital clue may well be that he had a visit in the afternoon from a lady whose daughter has been discovered to be in an interesting condition,' observed Peter. 'But I imagine that even *he* was a bit past it at his age. Let's try to summarise from memory, to see whether that helps to fix things. Forbes was at the meeting on Saturday night, with fifteen other people—'

'Sixteen including the Speaker, Prof Charleston—'

'But those sixteen include Bill Denny, who I cannot imagine having anything to do with it, Doctor Broad, who we've already met, the Lord Lieutenant, who must be above suspicion, and, I noticed two lesser members of the clergy and the Bishop himself. You don't think it's all part of a plot on the part of the Protestants, do you?'

'No, we'll leave them out, at least for now. Continue!'

'That leaves us with ten people to see. The Major arrived fairly late—he signed the book next to last of the Members. Taffy the Museum, Ivor Jones of Letchbury to you, signed last. Bill Denny was the only name on the guest page, and was introduced by him.

'The meeting heard the usual rehashed material about the Romans in the County, with new material from the speaker's own dig. Forbes asked a question about the relationship between the excavation the speaker had done at Water End and the Antonine Itinerary.'

'Explain that one, as if it matters,' interjected the Inspector.

'The Itinerary is a sort of Roman Milebook. It gave the distances between named places on a number of routes. Most of the routes are already worked out; the roads are known, as well as the stopping places. There are a few doubtful routes and unidentified stopping places, like a Villa

Faustini in East Anglia. I'd have to do my homework to find out what that might have to do with Broadshire, though. I thought that, as Bill said, all the juice had been squeezed out of that old lemon.'

'Go on with your summary,' ordered the Inspector.

'After the discussion, Forbes was seen to be circulating among the assembly, possibly trying to cadge a fiver or something. He was last seen by Bill Denny talking to Prof Charleston. He left the meeting late.'

'I've got to get back to the office and find out if the crime has been solved without me,' said the Inspector, pulling up outside Peter's front door. 'What do you propose to do next to help me?'

'I think I could do worse than take old Bill's advice. If I go to the Museum lecture tonight, I'm certain to be able to pick up some gossip for you, and I might even be able to talk to another of the members present at that fateful meeting. Taffy Jones is the speaker, so we can hope that I might get him aside afterwards.'

'I'll call for you if I can get away. What time is the meeting?'

'Eight o'clock. Be here at seven if you can make it; then we can have a quick jar of ale before we go.'

CHAPTER 8

The Museum lecture

Ken Harris was able to convince his superiors that he was off duty, or else that he was doing useful work in attending the lecture which had been organised by the Civic Society in Broadchester Museum. He called for Peter at seven o'clock, and they were soon ensconced in the snug of the *White Hart*, only a short distance from the Museum, to gather their resources and a little alcoholic stimulation before the meeting. Inspector Harris gave a brief résumé of the information that he had gathered from his minions, who had been collecting by 'routine enquiries' all day.

'We haven't been able to find anything unusual that happened to Forbes in the last week that could give a lead to his sudden demise. It appears he led a very quiet life, on his own at Gamekeeper's Cottage. His neighbours on both sides appear to be the original curtain tweakers and keyhole peekers. Both widows, with nothing much to do but bully the flowers in their small gardens. As far as we can tell, one or other, often both, of them was keeping an eye on the Major all last week. He was writing a book, a sort of popular account of excavations in the County. The manuscript was near his typewriter. I think it might have sold well—it had just the right blend of excitement over discovery and tourist content to satisfy the great Broadshire public. And believe it or not, he didn't go out farther than the postbox all week. His callers were the milkman, the baker, and the postman, apart from his housekeeper, who called every morning to make the bed, cook his lunch and clean up. She brought the provisions with her. There was no telephone at the cottage.

'My lads have found he was a most systematic old boy.

51

Kept a post book for incoming and outgoing mail. Letters awaiting attention all on a clip, others filed. No threatening letters, or anything like that; no personal messages for at least the last month, unless you count a postcard from Sienna with "The weather is fine we are looking for some more ruins love Squiggle",' said the Inspector dejectedly. 'He had a few bills, none of them for large sums, and a notice of the Archaeological Society meeting on Saturday.'

'How was his bank balance?' asked Peter.

'Nothing spectacular. He lived well within the income from his pension and writings. We did find a Post Office book that he had kept carefully for small deposits of rather odd sums. Your suggestion about the use of the well as a money mine seems to work out. All the peculiar deposits were made close to the times of full moons, and that bears out the fact that no-one saw any light at the Villa that night, or, indeed, any other night.'

'Did you check that he did indeed keep a record of all his mail?' said Peter, suddenly thinking of a possibility.

'The lad I had on that enquiry was nothing if not thorough. He managed to get the postman to recollect all the letters for the last two weeks, and his recollection tallies exactly with the Major's record,' the Inspector informed him, rather smugly.

'So, unless the crime, if crime it was, was premeditated, and planned a long time in advance, we must look for a motive at the meeting of the BAAAS, or at least that evening,' suggested Peter.

'You must remember, however, that if the murderer had spotted a clever way of committing the crime, and if he knew of the Major's descents into the depths after wealth, then he might have planned the whole thing and waited until his victim came along,' the Inspector pointed out.

'If someone had thought of a good way of doing the old boy in—and it must have been a good way or we'd have found out how it was done—why the blazes didn't he leave the ladder down the hole, so that we would think it was all an accident, and that Forbes had just collapsed, or slipped or something? I can't believe that anyone thinking this thing out would have made such a slip. Anyway, all you've got to look for is someone who has been unable to account for his movements every full moon since the Major made his last withdrawal. Which was—?'

'Sixteen weeks ago. Hmm! It appears that you have made your case. Unless the person in question only decided it was necessary to commit the crime in the last four weeks, he would have lain in wait for the victim at the full moon, and for some days either side of it,' said the Inspector. 'Not the sort of thing anyone would be likely to do without arousing suspicion.'

'Have you turned up any motive yet?' asked Peter. 'Did he have anything to leave, and if so, who would get it?'

'So far, it seems he died intestate. Next of kin is a cousin, who is at present in Brisbane. He will inherit a few pounds, and an old car; the cottage was rented and the Major's books on archaeology and related subjects go to the BAAAS,' said the Inspector with a gloomy face. 'No motive or opportunity there.'

'Uncovered any local gossip yet?'

'According to local gossip he was, as you might expect, obsessively mean. The only real scandal was a very old tale, years old, about Forbes living in a caravan on a site he was excavating, in sin with a local schoolma'am. She was supposed to be looking after his small finds, whatever they are. They were caught *in flagrante* by some of her senior pupils. Embarrassing—very. She left without giving notice. I think he was somewhat put off by the whole thing, and became more of a recluse. No *cherchez-la-femme* here.'

'We keep finding out that there is nothing to find out about him,' said Peter. 'You don't think he was blackmailing someone, say one of the County Antiques, who decided that it was time to "catch with this surcease success" after the meeting?'

'There's no supporting evidence as yet. No unexplained deposits in his bank account or anything like that.'

'We might discover that he was *about* to start blackmailing someone at the meeting, I suppose,' suggested Peter. 'We're back to a spur-of-the-moment type of crime again.'

'There is only one thing wrong with that—the actual moment chosen. How can you choose to commit a crime on the spur of the moment at midnight in an ancient monument? Not exactly the sort of place one just happens to be at that time, I would have thought. Hey! Come on, the meeting is due to start now.'

The Inspector drained his glass and they both hurried out into the dusk.

There were two museums in Broadshire. Neither of them was run by the County Council, the members of which begrudged even the money spent on the County Library Service. The museums were of contrasting types, reflecting as they did their peculiar origins. Letchbury Museum was owned by the Borough of that name, which had become rich almost overnight as the result of the decision of a local businessman to open up factories fit for people to work in. The factories were light inside, well ventilated, and hideous. The enlightened and illuminated Borough, which almost by chance found itself blessed with the wherewithall to satisfy the suddenly bourgeoning demand for its principal export, electrical appliances, before others had entered the field, also found itself almost embarrassed by its income. If, the burghers decided, the people work in pleasant surroundings, then we must make sure that they use their leisure in an enlightened manner. The result was 'The Institute', opened just before the turn of the century by one of the many offspring of the Queen, God bless her. The fact of the opening was recorded for all to see, in letters of gold, six inches high, on a polished marble slab eight feet square. Unfortunately, the inscription just belongs to that period when any permanent record was considered to be useless unless it was in a dead, and therefore immutable, language, Oxbridge Latin. That fact, and the fact that the offspring of the Queen were numerous, and the one delegated to perform the ceremony of cutting the ribbon with the scissors (still preserved in the collection, along with the spade used by the Prince Consort in planting a ceremonial tree nearby some years previously) was now forgotten, rendered the slab virtually useless, until the present curator realised its potential by labelling it as an exhibit, with a translation of the inscription to the last ablative absolute, and a family tree of the late Queen.

Letchbury Museum, then, being the product of enlightened times, was, of course, even more offensively hideous than the factories owned by the Vestal Electric Lamp Co. It was also very inconvenient. The first curator of the Museum had almost faced dismissal when he was heard to say that it was a pity that the money lavished on the exterior in adding those useless figures showing the great ladder of being, as revealed to Darwin, scrambling insanely over every jutty, cornice, frieze and coign of vantage, was not spent on the interior.

Not that the Museum failed, let it be said, to be light and well ventilated. Light, that was, if the products of the Vestal Electric Lamp Co. were always switched on, and well ventilated every time the doors were opened at either side of the building, as often happened during the school holidays.

By contrast, the Broadchester Museum, now owned by the municipality, was a result of a series of accidents. Its origin lay in the magpie instinct of two brothers, Ebeneezer and Phineas Deard, who began their unfortunate collection with a number of stuffed birds. The actual specimens have, fortunately, decayed into dust. Doubtless, as a result of the work of the brothers and their like, the actual species are threatened with extinction, if not already defunct. Not content with birds, they added a collection of mammals, rocks, fossils, bygones, knick-knacks, dolls-houses, tools and other unwanted paraphernalia. It has often been said that as regards accessions, that is, objects which enter a museum, there is only one door, and that door is marked 'Way in Only'. Objects bequeathed to the Museum, or loaned to the Museum, came in and there was no way of getting them out again. Even the things that had been lent to the collection, such as the model of Broadchester Cathedral made of God-knows-how-many matchsticks by a long departed aunt of a forgotten member of the Museum's Committee had become a fixture when it was realised that there was no known surviving member of the family to authorise its disposal.

The Broadchester Museum, unlike its rival in the industrial south, was not designed as anything so enlightened. It was, until the brothers Deard had obtained it, at the same time that they had helped to found the BAAAS, a timber-framed town house of the late sixteenth century. It had, in its early days, no pretence at display, and the accumulative work of Ebeneezer, Phineas, and their successors had been matched only by the erosive activities of the other occupants of the building, whose life cycle was maintained on energy to be derived from cellulose and lignin. The presence of the wood beetles was known and, as an inevitable concomitant of buildings of olde worlde charm, was tolerated.

The great stroke of luck for the city had come just after the last war, when it was decided that the building should be redecorated. The process began in the mineral gallery, which occupied the entire upper floor. In order to paint the walls, the decorators moved the collection into the centre of the floor. The resulting collapse, which was cumulative as the weight was added to the two floors below, served two remarkably fortunate purposes: it removed from active service the last of the unqualified octogenarian curators, and it enabled his successor—when the gutted building was restored with properly designed galleries—to write off a large part of the collection of junk.

The new galleries included a small lecture room. It had been designed for this purpose, which meant that it was insufficiently ventilated, and that it was furnished with plastic-seated chairs which, Ken was to find, insisted remorselessly that the interests of human anatomy should be subjugated, even mortified, in the interests of what the designer had inelegantly termed 'maximum stackability'. Lectures in this hall were a battle between visual elegance, (tasteful emulsion-painted walls, bright and colourful furnishings and concealed lighting), and extreme physical discomfort, caused by the lack of air and the procrustian chairs. The acoustics were awful.

When Harris and Wood arrived at the museum, it was a blaze of lights, and groups of people were standing around talking very loudly. Peter led Ken to a seat near the front of the lecture room. As they sat waiting for the meeting to begin, Peter gave his friend a short introduction to the situation in which he now found himself.

'This meeting is called by the Civic Society, who from time to time hold meetings to hear speakers on local topics. I say called. Perhaps that is too strong a word. I've never actually seen one of these meetings advertised anywhere. As you can see, the attendance is small,' (the Inspector counted twenty people in the audience) 'and consists of what the digging fraternity would call "old women of both sexes". Except that I see our friend Bill over there.' He waved. 'Ah! Here's our chairwoman, Mrs Fox, JP.'

Mrs Fox climbed up the steep steps onto the platform, accompanied by a small, wiry gentleman in his early thirties, with a neat pointed ginger beard. The lady was dressed in a navy blue suit, and was wearing a wide-brimmed felt hat, white with red flowers. As the platform party mounted the platform, there was a terrific disturbance at the back of the hall as an elderly gentleman, with a high-domed bald head, struggled in, carrying a folding table and a projector. The opening announcements, which the chairwoman made, were lost among the scraping of chairlegs on the parquet floor as a space was cleared among the chairs for the projectionist and his equipment.

'... which will be available after the meeting,' concluded the lady. 'Will you be long, Mr Bugg?'

'Not now, Mrs Fox, I've just got to get some power,' said the projectionist, beginning to string a cable along the tops of the curtain rails at one side of the hall, using a long pole with a hook on the end.

'Then we'll start, shall we? Good! Our speaker tonight, who is curator of the other museum in the county, the one at Letchbury, is, I am sure, already well known to you all for his work—'

'Scratching,' muttered Peter—

'—on archaeological sites throughout the county. He tells me he has lots of exciting discoveries to tell you all about tonight. He really needs no introduction from me. Ladies and gentlemen, Mr Ivan—er—' she hurriedly consulted a piece of paper, 'Ivor—that is—Jones.'

There was a scattering of applause as the speaker rose to his feet and stopped nibbling his fingernails. He began to speak very fast, pitching his voice uncomfortably high in his nervousness. He spoke with a lilting tone which betrayed his Cambrian origins.

'I think we'll begin with the first slide, if you don't mind, please, thank you very much.'

'Just a moment!' from the back of the hall. Everyone turned round, to see that the projectionist was busy with the plug on the end of a power cable, using a nailfile as a screwdriver. 'Just changing the plug! Blast the damn thing!' shouted the projectionist, dropping a small screw on the floor.

The speaker tried to get hold of the audience again, raising the pitch of his voice and its speed of delivery, as well as the volume.

'Never mind then, let's start with an introduction without the slides so that we can get on with it once we *have* the slides. My talk tonight is about my excavations on Windyridge, which lies on the top of the chalk escarpment which runs. . . .'

Behind the speaker, and on him, appeared a picture, so far out of focus as to be unintelligible. As one man the audience forgot what the speaker was saying as they held their breath, willing the picture into focus. The speaker lost the thread himself, and turned to watch, fascinated as the scene crawled into focus. It was a picture of a row of new houses.

'That's not one of mine, is it?' asked the speaker, faintly.

Suddenly the hall was plunged into darkness as all the lights were extinguished. The picture of the houses disappeared sideways, leaving the screen a blinding white. A map appeared. It was a familiar map of the County of Broadshire. Familiar except in one respect. The east and west were reversed. The speaker looked at it for a moment, and sang out, 'It doesn't really matter, we can make do with this!' and began to explain the position of his site in looking-glass land. He had no pointer, and stood on tiptoe, waving his arms towards the top of the screen. Suddenly the projectionist woke up to the error he had made, and the map slipped swiftly away. The audience gasped at the sudden glare as the screen was illuminated white again. The map reappeared with the west on the left, and the east on the right. The north was, unfortunately, at the bottom. The speaker launched higher and more rapidly into a guide to this new form of geography—and the screen was suddenly glaringly white again. Back came the map with the north point pointing towards the left-hand side. Glaring white again. The speaker waited, dumbfounded, as the remaining four possible positions for the slide were tried. It was at this point that Ken Harris became aware of the clashing sound of three ladies who were knitting with enormous wooden needles behind him, and the snores from his left.

Apart from the short break while the projectionist replaced a fused bulb, and the audience blinked at one another in the unexpected illumination, the lecture went quite well, and Taffy Jones settled down to a lucid account of excavation on a Neolithic site, with colourful and interesting pictures.

When the lights finally went up, the questions from the floor were confined to the usual small details, until Bill Denny rose to his feet to seek amplification of a point that Jones had evidently tried to gloss over, in deference to his audience. Denny was very persistent.

'Did I understand the speaker to say that during the dig he discovered a large chalk phallus?' he asked pianissimo.

'That is quite correct.'

'Could the speaker tell us where it was found?'

'It was in a hole in the centre of the eastern entrance to the camp.' The speaker sat down, and mopped his brow, glad to be out of that one. Denny rose again.

'In what position was this phallus found?'

The speaker stood up, and so far forgot himself as to make a gesture with his forearm.

'It was upright.'

'Doesn't the speaker think that this is very significant?'

CHAPTER 9

Taffy the Museum

After the lecture was over, Peter managed to wrest the speaker from a small knot of people, and guide him to the *White Hart* where he was met by Ken Harris, with pints of bitter already pulled, and Bill Denny, who seemed determined to join them. Harris was surprised to find that Denny and Jones appeared to be quite good friends.

'Cheers,' said Jones, raising his glass. Lowering it to rest on his knee, he addressed himself to Bill Denny. 'You mean bastard. You might have left my phallus alone!'

'As the bishop said to the actress. You shouldn't hide your cult object under a bushel,' he said with mock seriousness. 'That ruddy great penis of yours is the best thing that could have happened to Broadshire archaeology. Just what it needed to put a bit of masculinity into it. We ought to adopt it as a sort of emblem. If I'd found it, I'd go and wave it at the Society of Antiquaries!'

'Trouble with you, Billy my boy, is that you're a frustrated exhibitionist. You ought to go out with a plastic mac on, and expose yourself to the old women of the Civic Society. Dishonest, I call it, using a facsimile a few thousand years old. Like the quality Sunday newspapers, with their pseudo-medical articles as an excuse to expose a bit of tit in competition with their more popular rivals. Any excuse for a bit of eroticism, provided you can have it in the name of culture.' Taffy stopped abruptly and took a long draught from his beer.

'I'd like you to meet Ken Harris,' said Peter, taking advantage of the break in the banter. 'He's the copper who found that lovely mortarium that you've hidden in your basement somewhere.'

61

'Pleased to meet you. Sorry we can't find room to display everything. The trouble with the public is that they don't know how to use museums,' said Taffy.

'The trouble with the museums is that they don't put themselves out to find out what the public wants,' said Peter. 'What we've got you here for is so you can tell us all about last Saturday night's meeting of the BAAAS. You know that Major Forbes got himself killed after the meeting. Ken isn't happy about the circumstances of his death, and we're trying to piece together something of his last hours.'

'If you want the truth, you'll find her at the bottom of the well,' said Taffy, with unnecessary erudition. 'What can I tell you?'

'Tell us everything that happened at the meeting, as you remember it,' requested the Inspector, 'from when you arrived to when you left.'

'You don't expect me to remember what Prof Charleston said, I hope? Good. I arrived last. There were about twenty people there—'

'Sixteen. Go on.'

'Sixteen. That included Major Forbes. He arrived just in front of me. Billy here was waiting for me to sign him in as a visitor. I remember Tim Bugg (the other curator, the one from Broadchester) being there, and Dr Broad, and Doolittle-Smythe, and the Bishop and a couple of vicars. Lady Forster, the Lady President, took the chair. The paper was on Roman Broadshire. Nothing original in it, although it was the first time Charleston has shown the slides of the Water End dig outside Burlington House, as far as I know. After the talk there was very little discussion. The usual thing. People don't ask questions after papers at learned society meetings. They make little speeches about the parts of the lecture they think they understood, just to let everyone know they are there. The Bishop made quite a long sermon on the Roman tiles in the foundations of the Cathedral, I remember. Old Forbes asked something about

62

whether Water End had ever been considered as being one of the stages on *Iter* seventeen of the Antonine Itinerary. That's the main route through the county,' Taffy explained. 'There doesn't seem to be any doubt about where it goes. Most of it is under the main A7 road between Broadchester and Letchbury.'

'I see,' said Ken, 'Peter told me about the Itinerary yesterday. What happened after the questions were over?'

'The usual embarrassing vote of thanks, proposed at great length by Mark Petchy, the architect fellow. Carried by acclamation and all that, and then coffee and biscuits. Everyone on their best behaviour, you know, balancing food in their saucers and trying not to drop crumbs on their waistcoats. Circulating and being pleasant to the members of my Museums Committee who were there, including her ladyship.'

'Did you have a word with Major Forbes?' asked the Inspector.

'We met circulating in opposite directions. A short exchange about distribution of votive objects, religious things. Said he hoped I wasn't feeling too cramped in my museum now we had the finds from Windyridge. I laughed and said we'd always have room for anything he'd like to dig us up, even if I had to talk the Treasurer's Department into buying us a new gallery. He laughed and went off, saying that he would have a go at talking the BAAAS Council into giving him some money to finance a dig for me. Silly old duffer! God rest his Soul,' he added reverently, raising his glass, which had become full again.

'Did you notice when Forbes left, and who he left with?' asked Ken Harris.

'He was still there when I left,' said Taffy. 'He appeared to have buttonholed Charleston. They were in animated conversation when Billy here dragged me off to catch the last round before closing time.'

'Could I have your impression of Major Forbes, to add to

the others already given?' the Inspector asked Jones, as he managed to get him to one side, and the others were discussing digging.

'In confidence, yes. He was as straight as a die, physically and morally. At least as far as his own code went. I imagine he went in for a bit on the side in his youth, and that the ladies would have queued up for the privilege. He'd have lied like a gasmeter to keep a woman's name out of it, but otherwise he was honest as the day. He wasn't much of a man's man though, despite his military bearing. Too—ingratiating I think is the word. Always laid his hand on your arm when you were talking to him. Always stood just a little too close, so you were continually stepping back away from him. A bit of a pompous old ass, but a good archaeologist, because his reports were always so detailed and accurate.'

'Can you tell me anything about his close friends?' asked the Inspector.

'Now you come to ask it, I can't. Do you think the poor old thing had any? I don't think he was ever thick with anyone I knew of. What an odd life,' said Taffy. 'And what a dreadful obituary to have. Or an inscription for his tombstone: "In unloving memory, this stone was erected by his slight acquaintances". Oh dear.'

As the Inspector drove the archaeologist back home after the pub had closed, he admitted his deep depression over the case.

'Wasting the taxpayers' money again. We can't keep the coroner waiting, but this one hates formal evidence of identification followed by an adjournment. We haven't even got evidence of cause of death yet. I really don't think we got anything more from your friend the curator, do you?'

'Cheer up, old son,' said Peter. 'After all, think of all the nice people you are meeting. Really moving in the best circles, you are. But I agree with you; there's not a sniff of any reason for dirty work anywhere. We seem to have demolished the idea of a long-standing grievance, since no-one could have sat in wait for him on the offchance, without arousing suspicion, or at least a remark on their odd behaviour. I don't suppose you'd like to find an ingenious maniac who just happened along by chance, would you?'

'I'd love one,' agreed Ken Harris, 'and having met some of the County lot, I'm not so sure that you need to look for a madman happening along by chance. They're not the best circles really, are they?'

'They're all right if you like that sort of thing. But you haven't started prying into anyone's whereabouts at the time in question. And your enquiries about motive have been very softly, softly, haven't they? "Tell me, what was your impression of the deceased?" is rather mild as a way of finding out if they'd like to push him under a bus. You just haven't found anyone displaying any aggression against the old boy,' objected Peter.

Ken Harris showed the talent which had put him where he was; a talent for remembering scraps of dialogue, and for being able to organise them and rehearse them at a moment's notice.

'Your friend Dr Broad said he was "a straightforward military type ... no complications ... very good director ... everything according to the drill book". He "couldn't remember his ever being associated with any other member" and "never knew him that well". I suppose you can't say he hated him from that, but it's pretty cold praise of someone so respected.

'I didn't ask Bill Denny what he thought directly, but he gave a very good impression of him. Called him "fierce and friendly", "pompous" and "a mean old basket". I got the distinct impression that he secretly admired him.'

'I think we *all* did, in a sort of way,' Peter put in. 'He was a good director, whatever anyone says. His reports were excellent. We might all be a bit jealous of his good public relations. He appears to have been a great success, until we try to find his friends.'

'You didn't overhear what Ivor Jones said, but he agreed with you—"a bit of a pompous ass, but a good archaeologist. His reports were detailed and accurate".'

'That sounds like one of my end-of-term reports,' exclaimed Peter. 'What else did he say?'

'That he was "straight as a die, physically and morally", apart that is from his sex life, which it was suggested was concluded some time ago. He also said he was "not a man's man; too ingratiating. Always stood too close". Again I can see there someone admiring someone he didn't like,' recalled Ken. 'When I asked Taffy what friends the Major had, he suggested an inscription for his tombstone; "In unloving memory, this stone was erected by his slight acquaintances", Taffy did seem upset by the idea, but he really meant it.'

They pulled up outside Peter's house. Peter got out of the car.

'I shan't invite you in for supper,' he said. 'I expect you have a busy day tomorrow. Anyway, you've already drunk a hearty meal. You'll probably either turn up the motive or the murder weapon tomorrow.'

'I don't know about the motive, but there's no weapon to be found as far as I can see. We don't know what we're looking for, but we've gone over the whole area inside and outside the Cold Beech Roman Villa with the proverbial fine tooth comb. There's nothing to be found there, I'm sure of that,' asserted the Inspector, rashly.

The fact that he was wrong was discovered the next day. It was one of those chance discoveries, and Peter often wondered whether the truth would have dawned on anyone if he had not happened to be there with Ken at the time. It was chance that he was there, and it was chance that the discovery was made that particular day. Altogether the stars must have smiled on the policeman that Tuesday. With murder confirmed, the enquiries could take a harder line.

CHAPTER 10

How it was done

Tuesday brought no change in the mellow autumn weather, and Peter was very glad to be going back to visit Cold Beech Villa, and the little hamlet of Natford which was its near neighbour across the fields. Although there were still several people who were at the BAAAS meeting who had not been interviewed, Detective Inspector Kenneth Harris was in a perambulating mood, and was not to be hurried.

'It's all very well getting these constables plodding around filling in questionnaires and so on,' he told Peter, as they left the car in the park next to the *Fisherman's Rest*. 'What we both need to do, you as an archaeologist and I as a detective, is to make a pilgrimage to the scene of the crime. Reports are one thing, but actual topography is another.'

They set out in companionable silence along the road. The hamlet (it didn't warrant the name village, having no church of its own) was just a small cluster of cottages, and the pub. Gamekeeper's Cottage, which was the first object of their pilgrimage, was a little back from the road, where a track entered the park to some distant and unseen hall. It at once became clear that when the police had said that the Major's neighbours on either side had kept him under close observation, they were quite right in inferring that he had had no comings and goings without their knowledge, at least during the day. The neighbouring cottages were on either side of the track, facing inwards. The track made a right-angled bend and went past the front of the Major's cottage, which therefore looked out between its neighbours at the main road. The tracks ended at high gates into the park, which were padlocked.

67

'To get to or from the Major's cottage, one would have to run the gauntlet of the two ladies on either side,' said the Inspector. 'Good morning!' (This to one of the neighbours, who popped up from behind the hedge, holding a bunch of dead blooms). 'See what I mean?' (Dropping his voice again). 'Unless one had a key to the padlock on the gates. And then you'd be in full sight of the others as you came through it, and walked up his garden path. If he had any visitors it must have been at dead of night.'

They walked slowly along the track to the gates, stared at Gamekeeper's Cottage, and walked slowly back. Neighbour on the right was still in the garden, lurking behind some late dahlias. Neighbour on the left was visible as a slight movement of a lace curtain at a lower window.

'I hope you didn't want to go in and pry?' asked the Inspector.

'Not at all. I always feel uncomfortable when people ask me into their privy chambers when I didn't know them well. Going in without an invitation is just not done—even if there is no-one alive to object,' said Peter.

'You'd never make the grade as a detective, would you? Let's go to see Mrs Weston, who used to "do" for the Major. I feel we ought to drop in and see her, in case she's feeling a bit neglected now. I imagine she must have gone over there more for company, and for something to do, than for the little bit she got for the job. Ah, this must be the place.'

He turned in at a narrow front gate, and they went up a short flight of steps. Sitting on the steps was a tortoise-shell cat. Sitting in an armchair on the lawn beside the path, also enjoying the mellow rays of the September sun, was a very old man. He had that shrunken appearance which comes with senescence, as if the skeleton inside were asserting itself. His healthy complexion belied this. He was as brown as a cob nut in October, and his bright blue eyes twinkled at them.

'We've come to see Mrs Weston,' said the Inspector, and

then raised his voice, as the old man put his head on one side, like a bird, without replying. 'MRS WESTON?'

The old man pointed silently towards the front door of the house, which stood open. They approached it, and a cheerful voice from inside bade them enter.

The door opened straight into the front parlour, which was a joy for Peter to behold. It should, he thought, have been scheduled for preservation. An inventory of its contents should be sent to some archive for research. Quite clearly Mrs Weston was a collector; not in the antiques and bygones sense that the word has today, but in a much simpler sense. She had trinkets and knick-knacks that she had bought or been given on every ledge and sill, and pictures large and small covering the walls. A closer look revealed that many of the objects had probably been left to her by older friends and relations, and that she had been able to part with nothing. And all the frames, all the Goss porcelain, and all the brass and glass shone.

As they passed through the front door, Mrs Weston was coming with short, rapid steps through the other door of the room, wiping her hands on her apron. She was, they discovered, a collector's piece herself. Her age was difficult to guess, although Peter would have hazarded that she would never see seventy again. Her taste in clothing, he imagined, had tended to stick with the fashions of her youth, in the twenties or thirties of the century. She was wearing a loose fitting dress heavily patterned in dark-coloured flowers, lisle stockings, buckle shoes with heavy block heels, and a long double string of artificial pearls. The thickness of her steel-rimmed spectacles indicated that she suffered from long sight, but her movements were active, bustling, and firmly accurate. They had to be as she picked her way among her treasures, dusting and polishing.

'You'll be needing a cup of tea, won't you? I've just put it on. I've got some fresh seedy cake in the larder. Not shop-bought seedy cake, that would never do, would it? But the

69

real thing, just like my mother used to make. She won prizes with her seedy cake did my mother. I've never actually won any prizes with mine, mostly because I haven't ever entered it in the show. Well, you see, my Charlie, him what you just met outside, deaf as a post he is, loves it so much that he always cuts a slice from it before it's had time to cool down. So I never get around to having a cake to take to the show when show day comes.'

Even the experienced Inspector Harris was a little taken aback by the friendly and open way they were accepted into the house, and, with an effort, he broke into the flow to introduce himself. The fact that they were engaged in investigating the death of her friend and employer diverted the torrent a little. Peter recognised the type. He knew that the lady would not be susceptible to mere logic. This was the stuff that rumours were made of. If she made her mind up about something, no demonstration of the fact that it wasn't true would change the story she would tell.

'You'll be wanting to know all about the Major then. Such a pity it was that he should go and have that accident just as he was getting on so well with his book about his work. Can't think what he was thinking of, going down there at that time of night. Catch his death, that's what he might have done,' she babbled, with unconscious irony. 'I expect he went down there to remind himself of something about the place when he was in charge of the digging there. It must have been an accident, because he couldn't have done it himself, and he didn't have no enemies so no-one else could have done it. I don't hold with these people who gossip about a poor man like the Major. He hadn't got anybody to look after him, poor soul, and he was such a nice man. And so clever too. He knew things that no-one else had ever thought of. And he's been as good as gold after that trouble with Miss Tonks from the school. Proper training ground for criminals that place is. Calls itself a comprehensive school. Used to call places like that approved schools when I was a girl. And those boys shouldn't have been poaching down by the excavations then they wouldn't have seen nothing to shock theirselves. Not that they could have been shocked anyway, the way they carry on at that place. Why do you know . . .' and so the stream of speech flowed on to the second cup and the last crumb of seedy cake.

With some difficulty they extracted themselves, Peter promising he would come back to be told 'all about the diggings'. As they walked away down the road, Kenneth wiped his brow with a handkerchief.

'Do you still think she feels lonely and neglected then?' asked Peter.

'I reckon old Forbes did it himself to escape. It was either that or go deaf like her Charlie.'

'To the Villa now?' asked Peter.

'Shall we take the car?'

'Oh, fat detective whom nobody loves, why do you drive to the crime in gloves?' Peter misquoted. 'The trouble with you thoroughly modern coppers is that you are always "missing so much and so much". I'm sure that more accidental discoveries of crime are made by archaeologists than by the police. Do you remember that time we found that safe hidden in the chalk pit? In the old days one of your blokes would have seen it straight away. Nowadays they chug past on their little noddy bikes and see nothing. We'll walk. This way,' and he turned through a gap in the hedge.

'Blow me!' ejaculated the Inspector. 'I never knew we could come through here.' It was only a very short walk, across two fields, and jumping a small stream, to the structure which covered the Cold Beech Roman Villa.

'See what you miss by being wheelbound. I wouldn't mind betting you even money that Freddy Forbes came this way to his doom on Saturday night, or early Sunday morning. Surely everyone knows this short cut? It's all right when the weather's dry, as it has been lately, but you'd need your big wellyboots if it was wetter. Come November, you'll be up to your knees in clag down here by the stream. Just now it's as hard as rock right down to the water.'

'We just don't have village coppers like we used to,' Harris complained. 'You're quite right. In the old days we'd have been told by the local man all about the local geography. Put in the picture properly. Think what we might have missed because we didn't know about this path. There might have been an essential clue down here somewhere. It wouldn't have been footprints though. You're right about the hard ground.'

They stopped by the little stream, which ran between high banks except at the crossing place, where the banks were lower and the water a little wider. It was quite easy to jump there nevertheless, and there was little vegetation to impede the crossing as there was at other places. The cottages of Natford could clearly be seen behind them, and the building covering Cold Beech Villa in front of them, lurking among the trees.

'You can't put Blacky, who is in charge of the Villa, into our main categories of archaeologists. Simple fact is, he is a custodian, not a curator. All the world of difference as far as *they* are concerned. He has no qualifications except those needed by the Inspectorate of Ancient Monuments to look after their property. He doesn't dig, theorise or curate. He just custodes. Must be honest and British,' explained Peter, as they walked up to the front door of the Villa.

The scene inside the structure provided by the enlightened Inspectorate of Ancient Monuments to cover this particular Custodianship Site had changed very little since the morning of the discovery of the body. It still looked, Peter thought to himself, more like a modern school swimming pool than a Roman building, until you realised that instead of water down the middle there were flint and mortar foundations, and rather dry looking mosaic floors.

It had always seemed a pity that the new structure had so

72

completely destroyed the atmosphere that the site had seemed to possess when they had been digging it all those years ago. It seemed even more surprising, somehow, that the atmosphere was unchanged by the mysterious death which had occurred there a couple of days before. It was true that the people walking around up on the raised platforms, which permitted them to look down on the remains of a once sumptuous Roman house, were talking quietly as if they were in a place of worship, but then, he knew, that is always the effect of anything that claims to be cultural. Educated people never raise their voices in hallowed places like libraries, concert halls, museums, and public conveniences.

Mr Black, the custodian, was sitting at the little counter beside the door from which he dispensed tickets, guidebooks, postcards and slides. He was an elderly man, probably past retiring age in any more active job. He had a thin face, with veins close to the surface; he wore bifocal spectacles with thick sidepieces, like blinkers, and a small Charlie Chaplin moustache. His clothing was Ministry issue; over his white shirt and dark tie he was wearing a grey alpaca jacket, with golden royal crowns in the lapels. His official peaked cap, with shiny brim and crown badge lay on the desk. He never wore it, but they sent him a new one every year for display. He stood up when he saw them come in, and offered his hand to the Inspector, who shook it warmly.

'Hello, Inspector. Have you discovered who was here with the Major on Saturday night?' he asked.

'Not yet,' admitted the Inspector. 'I was wondering whether you might have thought of anything which might help us. I understand that you weren't at all surprised that the Major had a key to the Villa?'

'I didn't know that he had one, but it didn't really surprise me. You remember that he was the director of this excavation all those years ago. When the building was put up over the top, he was still working here, and he acted as a sort of adviser to the Ministry. He often used to bring parties of visitors to see the site, and I suppose that he arranged to have a key cut for his own use at that time. I've only been here for a couple of years myself.'

'Can you tell us anything at all about the Major. What sort of person was he?' asked the Inspector.

'I didn't know him well. He only came in once or twice while I was here. You know what he looked like and all that. He sort of behaved as he looked. Every bit the retired officer. He was always very pleasant, but, well, you know—a snob,' answered the custodian.

'When was he here last, as far as you know?'

'I imagine it was the BAAAS visit,' said the custodian, opening a large diary from a drawer under the counter. 'April 5th.'

'Thanks. May we look round?' asked the Inspector.

'Help yourself.'

They walked slowly round the Villa, with Peter explaining the site to his friend, and adding little snippets of information, and reminiscences of the actual excavation not usually to be found in guidebooks. They had just reached the highest platform overlooking the remains, when Peter idly noticed a man in a blue uniform carrying a clipboard with a sheaf of papers on it come through the door.

'Is he one of yours?' he asked Ken Harris.

The Inspector turned and looked down.

'Nothing to do with me,' he replied. 'Fire brigade. They go round from time to time checking things like emergency doors, fire-escapes, hydrants and so on, in public buildings and factories.'

They watched as the fireman stood below them and looked around. He seemed satisfied, and wrote busily on his clipboard. Then he went over to a row of buckets of sand. He dug his hand into one bucket, as if he doubted that it could be sand all the way down.

'They're clean. Had my lads empty them and fill them up again,' the Inspector muttered in Peter's ear.

The fireman then took an object from his pocket, picked up a fire extinguisher from a bracket on the wall, and attached it to the object, and allowed it to hang from his extended arm.

'A spring balance,' thought Peter. 'Weigh them to see if they're full. Simple.'

He continued to explain the pattern on a mosaic floor to his companion. He observed without interest as the fireman wrote on his board and on the extinguisher itself, and moved on round the Villa, trying the emergency doors and testing other extinguishers. The fireman went out of the door, carrying one of the extinguishers, only to return shortly with it and replace it on its bracket. He wrote on his clipboard again, and went out of the door, stopping to get Mr Black to sign one of the papers on the clipboard.

Ken Harris was astonished when Peter Wood suddenly galvanised into action.

'Stop that man!' he shouted. 'Help! Fire!'

He sprinted for the top of the steps that led from the platform, and almost fell down them in his haste. The detective was a little slow off the mark, but hurried in his wake. He had almost caught him up as he burst out into the sunshine. There was a small blue van leaving the car park beside the Villa. The Inspector saw it had the Broadshire coat of arms on the side. Peter just managed to beat the van onto the road, and stood in its path, forcing it to stop. The driver wound down his window.

'What the blazes do you think you're doing, rushing out like that?' asked the fireman, who was driving.

'What have you just been doing in there?' panted Peter.

'Just a routine check on the fire appliances and so on. What's it got to do with you, may I ask?' said the fireman, in a surly voice.

The Inspector produced a warrant card.

'Detective Inspector Harris, Broadshire Constabulary,' he said, in a most imposing manner. 'I have reason to believe that you may be able to help me with enquiries I am making into a certain matter. Might I have a word?'

While the fireman was parking his van by the side of the road, the Inspector hissed at Peter, 'You'd better tell me what all this is about—quick.'

Peter replied.

'Just you ask him what he just did. He's just found out how the deed was done, and smuggled the evidence out under your very nose.'

The fireman joined them, carrying his clipboard.

'Can you tell us, briefly, what you have just been doing in there?' asked the Inspector.

'A routine check of the fire precautions, that's all. We do one every three months. Check visually, wiring and so on—make sure no-one's been tampering or altering, no worn wires. Check escapes, make sure routes are free from obstructions. Check devices like hoses, buckets, extinguishers. Just routine, really.'

'Did you find anything wrong today?' Peter took over the interrogation.

'It's always O.K. at Cold Beech,' replied the fireman. 'Blackie always keeps the firebuckets clear of fag-ends, and the exits unobstructed. The only thing that was wrong was one of the extinguishers. It had been let off, or perhaps it had leaked. Anyway, it was empty. I replaced it.'

'Wouldn't it make a mess, leaking like that?' asked the Inspector.

'Oh no. With the valuable objects they have in there, the instructions were that the hand appliances, the "first aid" things that would be used first before the water hoses were deployed, would be see oh two. Less mess, and safer with all the electric wiring they are. If the fire could be put out with them, there'd be no messing up the place.'

'What is a see oh two extinguisher?' asked Harris,

76

temporarily bewildered.

'Carbon dioxide. It's a gas. Smothers the fire,' replied the fireman.

'We'll have to take the extinguisher that you removed,' said Peter, playing the part of assistant to the Inspector with confidence. 'The Inspector here will give you a receipt. We'll arrange to come and take a statement from you shortly. Just a brief statement to the effect that you changed the extinguisher, where it was, and why you did it. Will you be at the station this afternoon? Good. We'll send a man along.'

Peter took the extinguisher, a red cylinder, like an overgrown bulb for refilling a soda syphon, carefully by its top, which was rather like a gun with a trigger, and a black barrel which was a simple narrow cone, like a toy trumpet. He held it with his handkerchief, as if it were hot.

The Inspector and the archaeologist retraced their steps across the fields.

'All right. I know carbon dioxide is a poisonous gas. He wasn't poisoned though,' insisted the Inspector. 'Anyway, you don't think my doctor would miss a simple thing like poisoning, do you?'

'It held four pounds of CO_2,' said Peter, half to himself. 'I see. It's not a poison. It smothers. It doesn't even do that to people, I don't suppose; at least not straight away. When you get a whiff of it, what it makes you do is breathe hard. The process which naturally goes on in your lungs is that the oxygen is taken from the air, and the carbon dioxide which your muscles and so on produce, is given out. When you breathe out, you expel lots of the gas. It's the CO_2 in your lungs that *makes* you breathe out, in fact. You know what a struggle you have to "hold your breath".'

'Go on. You interest me,' said Harris.

'Anaesthetists use CO_2 when they want to excite the patient to breathe harder. I imagine if you had an old man, like Forbes was, standing in water, and he got a good dose of the gas, he might well collapse, particularly if he was a bit

77

asthmatic. He wouldn't be gassed. He'd fill his lungs with water, and drown instead.

'Two pounds of carbon dioxide is, let me think,—about 1,800 grammes, or 900 litres. Dammit, can't remember how many litres there are in a cubic foot. Doesn't matter. Let's say the well was a metre and a half across. . .' The archaeologist reverted to his science master's role in silence for the rest of the walk across the fields. Then he suddenly emerged from his reverie.

'If you poured it carefully, I think it would make a layer about three feet deep above the water in the well. I suppose it would mix with the air and actually form a deeper layer than that in practice. Four feet deep would be enough for the purpose.' He held up the extinguisher. 'Exhibit A, the murder weapon.'

CHAPTER 11

A harder line

When the detective and the archaeologist reached the car, they very carefully put the large red cylinder into a plastic bag, and laid it on the back seat.

'That'll give the boys in the lab something to play with. Not that they can expect anything from it really, but they ought to go through the motions. I bet if it has any fingerdabs on it, they'll belong to everyone but the murderer,' said the Inspector.

'One thing we have achieved this morning, is that we can now speak of murder with a fairly confident tone,' put in Peter. 'That does mean that your questioning can be a bit more direct. You're not dissatisfied about the cause of death now. I suppose the correct cliché is that you "have reason to believe" that his death was due to miching malecho.'

'Yes,' agreed Ken Harris. 'That's a relief. With a time of death fairly confidently established, and method of killing pretty well outlined, it looks as if we can take a stronger line with our interviews. No-one can object to being asked where he was at the material time, for instance. The only question now is, who do we ask for their alibis?'

'I still think it must have something to do with the meeting on Saturday night. Anyway, we haven't got a line on anyone else yet,' said Peter.

'There is an interesting line of enquiry into that rather stale tale about what the archaeologist said to the schoolteacher. We ought to find out whether she went gracefully out of his life, and whether there might be some delayed repercussions. Not very likely after all this time. We can get her local police station to check her out, and also make enquiries at the school where she worked. What was its name?'

'Don't know. Ma Weston said it "called itself a comprehensive school". Let's look it up,' Peter suggested, getting back out of the car and crossing the car park to the telephone box next to the pub. Luckily the telephone books were intact. He picked up the one labelled Broadshire and opened it at 'S' for Schools. No help, so he turned to Broadshire County Council. About three columns of fine print met his gaze. He ran his eye quickly down these. Eventually, right at the end of the entries, he found what he was looking for: 'Schools—see under name of school'.

He looked up to the dialling instructions in the box and dialled 100. After a long wait, a voice answered,

'Number please?'

'Could I have directory enquiries, please?' asked Peter.

There was another long period of ringing tone.

'Which town?' asked a girl's voice.

'Broadchester. Could you tell me the name and address of the local comprehensive school, please?'

'What is its address?'

'I don't know, that's why I'm asking you.'

'I'm sorry, caller. I cannot help you unless you can supply more information.' The line went dead.

Peter was about to risk another discussion with Mrs Weston, when the mobile library hove into view. He flagged it down, and got the information that he wanted. He went back to the car and told Ken.

'Mayor's Walk School. It's just outside Broadchester on this road.'

'Probably a waste of time to go there during the holidays. Still, we might find a school secretary in, and it's on our way.'

As they drove along, they planned their campaign for the rest of the day. Ken would have to go back to the mysterious depths of his office to check up on the routine enquiries, as well as to hot them up now that murder seemed certain. Then they would go round and try to see all the rest of the people who were at the meeting, and see if they could find out what might have happened afterwards, and why.

'There were sixteen people present other than the victim. We've only met three of them so far. Messrs Broad, Denny and Jones. The Lord Lieutenant we've agreed to leave out, along with the Bishop and two parsons. That leaves nine. We'll have to get a wiggle on and see all these people. Just a check on their whereabouts at the time in question should be enough to clear them. But we really want them to give us a lead,' summarised the Inspector.

A further ten minutes driving brought them to Broadchester's outskirts, and to the school they wanted to see. They drove in through the gates.

'Stop a mo'!' shouted Peter. Ken braked hard. 'Back up a bit.'

They stopped by a sign which read:

'mayors walk school headmaster g d hanbury m a'

'Cripes!' said the Inspector fervently. 'Do you think they teach punctuation in there?'

'Haven't you noticed the great coincidence?' asked Peter. 'Get out that list of people you want to interview. There you are—"G D Hanbury". Perhaps our luck has changed.'

The school was so large that the roads which served its glass-sided buildings were provided with a one-way system. Eventually they reached the car park, which was empty. They got out, and went straight into the imposing double doors in front of them. They found themselves in the kitchen. There was nobody there. They emerged again and walked around, peering into windows to get a clue as to where they might most profitably go. Suddenly they were confronted by a large man with a very short, almost shaven, haircut. He was wearing a brightly flowered shirt, and jeans.

'We're looking for the headmaster,' explained the Inspector.

'Who is "we"?' asked the man, rudely.

'I'm Detective Inspector Harris, of the County Constabulary—'

'And I'm the King of Siam. Now clear off. This is private property and you're trespassing!'

Ken quickly produced his warrant card, and waved it in front of the ruffian's face.

'Can you tell us, please, where we can find the headmaster?' he asked.

'*I'm* the headmaster. Perhaps we'd better go to my study.' The man turned and led them into one of the buildings.

The detective and the archaeologist followed the burly figure of the headmaster through the long corridors of the empty school, which smelt strongly of cheap floor polish. Eventually, they were led into a room marked 'Headmaster'.

The room was enormous, with glass walls on two sides giving an extensive view of asphalt playground and grass playing fields. In the distance a tractor with a gang mower was cutting the grass, and a small gang of four men with ladders were making a great show of erecting a set of goalposts.

'How can I help you, gentlemen?' asked the headmaster, arranging the investigators in leather armchairs, so that they faced him over an immense desk with a plate glass top, which was almost in the middle of the deep-piled orange carpet. The top of the desk was bare except for three telephones. Peter wondered what the red phone was for. Could it be the hot line to the local crime squad?

'We are making enquiries, and wonder if you could help us with some information,' said the Inspector, rather vaguely.

'What are the enquiries about?' replied the headmaster, bluntly. 'I don't give information unless I know what its prospective use is likely to be.'

'It is a murder enquiry,' admitted the Inspector, for the first time making use of the dreadful phrase, 'and you are only involved indirectly, but, I think, in two ways. The dead man was Major Forbes. I believe he was a friend of one of your staff here some time ago. A Miss Tonks.'

'Miss Tonks? I'm afraid she left us some time ago,' said the headmaster.

'We already know that. But she does seem to be one of the few persons we have been able to trace so far who had any connection with the Major,' explained the Inspector.

Rather unexpectedly, the headmaster's face broke into a broad smile. Then he chuckled.

'Connections might appear to be the understatement of the year, if what I heard at the time was anywhere near the truth. She used to help him on his digs, often staying after the others had gone home. As I understand it, some of the pupils at the school were near one of these excavations late one evening, and caught the Major and the schoolma'am "having connections" as you so felicitously put it *en plein air*. Very enjoyable, but bad for discipline. We managed to get her moved on to another education authority forthwith. For the record she had a breakdown, and when she recovered she was fixed up with employment elsewhere. Devon, it was. Glad to get rid of her, actually. Bit of a nympho, if you ask me. Caught her in the stock cupboard with one of the art teachers at a Christmas party for the Common Room. After the incident with the Major, I was told in confidence that the senior master was certain that she was using the domestic science rooms for immoral purposes.'

'You don't think that the affair with the Major was, shall we say, serious?' asked the Inspector. 'I mean, she would be unlikely to feel any resentment towards the Major that he didn't make an honest woman of her?'

'Being made honest was the last thing she would have wanted,' the headmaster replied, with a smile. 'She was promiscuous.'

'You say she went to Devon. I shall have to get her called

upon by one of the local CID, just to check up,' said the Inspector.

'Make sure he's an experienced married man then!' joked the headmaster.

'There is one other way in which you can help us, if you would,' the Inspector went on, 'and that is by telling us what happened at the BAAAS meeting on Saturday night. I don't imagine anything unusual went on,' he added hastily, when he saw the puzzled look on the headmaster's face. 'It's just that the meeting was the last time the Major was seen in public, and we are trying to get a line that might tell us how he came to be killed shortly afterwards. Can you give us a brief account of the meeting?'

'Certainly. We were addressed by Prof Charleston, a very fine scholar indeed. A very thoughtful paper on Roman Broadshire. Very interesting indeed.'

'Did you happen to notice the Major there by any chance?' asked the Inspector.

'One cannot—or I should say could not—help noticing the Major. He was a very persistent and ingratiating person. He asked a question at the end of the meeting, about the Antonine Itinerary. He asked about the possibility of Water End being one of the *Mansiones*. He seemed quite cocky about the idea. Charleston demolished him quite quickly by reciting the names of the stages and the distances—all off by heart. No mean feat. Then he pointed out that the route of that particular *iter* was well established already.'

'What happened after the questions?' asked the Inspector.

'We had coffee as usual. I saw old Forbes pottering round chatting. I escaped early, so I didn't speak to him,' the headmaster replied.

'Just one last question,' said the Inspector, 'which I hope you won't resent; we must ask everyone involved. Where were you after the meeting, until dawn?'

'In bed with my wife. You ask her. She enjoys it.' The headmaster rose, and escorted them from the building.

CHAPTER 12

A gaggle of antiques

Peter had a quick lunch on his own in a public house in Broadchester, and then whiled away his time in the local library, while Ken was busy setting a full-scale murder enquiry in motion. In the library he spent his time trying to find out more details of the Roman occupation of Broadshire, and about the Antonine Itinerary, so that he could be better informed about the subject of the last meeting that Major Forbes had attended when he discussed it with the people who had been present. As he had expected, he found very little of interest to him. The last comprehensive information on the county was in the Victoria County History, which had been produced fifty years before, when the standard of scholarship was much higher than the standards of field archaeology. The information he gained did serve to augment his already considerable knowledge of the subject, however.

He had arranged to meet Ken at the library. When the Inspector came in he appeared in great spirits.

'Well, at least we are doing something definite now. We're not pussyfooting around saying that we are not satisfied about this death. We are looking for the man who pulled the trigger. Nothing on the murder weapon of any use to us. Only one set of prints, and they must belong to the fireman.'

Noticing the disapproving stares from the other users of the reference library, Peter steered the Inspector out into the street. The Inspector went on talking.

'I've sent men out to get routine statements from the people we have already seen, and to ask them to account for their movements at the time of the murder,' he continued, 'and I've found out which of the people at that meeting were clergy. I think we can give them a miss, at least for the present. And the Lord Lieutenant. We still have eight people to interview. We'll make notes as we go on now, so that the statements are easier to produce.'

He thrust a regulation notebook into Peter's hand. 'I hope you don't mind being seconded into the Force,' he added, 'and that you can take the notes fast.'

They walked round the corner, and the Inspector dislodged a rather disappointed traffic warden who didn't recognise the police registration number. Peter explained to the poor woman that it was a well-known fact that a police car was incapable of causing an obstruction, even when parked on a yellow line.

As they entered Broadchester Museum for the second time in the investigation, the bells of the Cathedral announced the hour of three, and the message was repeated by other clocks over the town. The Museum looked neglected when seen in daylight. Peter led the way to a door marked 'Curator'. He knocked. There was no reply. He knocked again. Still no answer. He tried the door.

'You can't go in there, that's private, that is: that's the curator's office!' snapped an unexpected voice from behind them. They turned. The corridor was empty. The voice went on, 'He hasn't got back from his lunch yet, so you can't see him.'

Peter located the voice to a small trap in the opposite wall, like a ticket office at a railway station. Through the window an elderly lady, with dishevelled hair, was peering at them short-sightedly. The Inspector braved the powerful aroma of tom cats which appeared to emanate from the window, and assumed his most charming manner.

'Good afternoon, Mrs—'

'—Miss! Miss Spratt,' she corrected.

'We were hoping to see Mr Bugg, Miss Spratt,' said the Inspector, 'but perhaps you can help us a little while we wait.' He looked carefully in the small notebook that he

86

always carried. 'I think you may have been at the meeting of the BAAAS last Saturday evening?'

'That's right. I'm always there. Someone has to make the coffee. You can't expect any of them to do that, so I always goes along with Mr Bugg. He does the slides,' she explained, 'while I brews up.'

'I wonder then, whether you can tell us anything about the meeting?' asked the Inspector.

'Thinking of joining, was you? You has to be proposed and seconded and all that, you know. By real members. You can't just join,' she added, 'like it was a club or something.'

'No, we're police officers,' said the Inspector, including Peter with a wave of his hand.

'Oooh! Did somebody pinch something?' she enquired.

'No, this is just a routine enquiry,' the Inspector replied. 'Something happened on Saturday night, and we think that perhaps someone at the meeting may have noticed something which might help us.'

'Well, I wasn't at the meeting. At least, I was and I wasn't, in a manner of speaking,' Miss Spratt replied, rather flurried. 'You see, I keeps in my little kitchen until I hears the applause. Then I wheels on the coffee. So I don't know much about what goes on. Then I'm so busy that I still don't have time to notice nothing.'

'Did you see Major Forbes at the meeting?' asked the Inspector.

'Yes, he was there. I remember he asked me, joking like, if I would come and make coffee for him at his new dig.'

'New dig? Was he doing one then?' asked Peter.

'I don't know. I didn't think he meant it,' said Miss Spratt, dismally. Peter thought that was the story of her life. 'Here comes the curator now!' she said, and banged the trap shut, cutting them off.

Mr Bugg was the elderly man, with the high, domed, bald head, who had been working the projector at the meeting Peter and Ken had attended at the Museum the night before.

He already knew Peter from previous occasions when he had made enquiries at the Museum, and had given museum lectures. He shook him limply by the hand.

'Hello, Mr Wood. Can I help you?' he asked, in a surprisingly deep voice.

'Well, it's Inspector Harris that wants your help, actually,' Peter admitted. 'Can you spare a moment?'

'We're terribly busy in the Museum at the moment,' Mr Bugg replied, apparently seriously, 'but come in.'

He ushered them into his office, which was a very large room. 'Almost,' Peter remarked later to Ken, 'as big as the display space in the Museum.' It held a large desk, and a larger table. Both items of furniture, as well as the windowsills, were covered with papers, some in files, and some loose. From among the papers, objects occasionally projected, a stuffed bird here, a stone there, a horse's jawbone over there, and so on.

'Do sit down,' said the curator, taking papers off two chairs, and dumping them on the floor. 'Now what is the nature of your enquiry?'

'I'm afraid it's a murder enquiry, Mr Bugg,' said the Inspector. 'We believe that Major Forbes was murdered on Saturday night. We are therefore anxious to trace his last movements, to find out how he met his end. Can you tell us all about the meeting on Saturday night. Everything that happened. It may give us a lead.'

Mr Bugg pondered.

'I arrived early, to set up the projector and screen. I had a chat with Mr Doolittle-Smythe while the others were coming in. The speaker arrived with Mrs Duguid, I think; he brought the slides to me, and explained which way they were arranged. Lady Forster introduced him. His talk was about Roman Broadshire. Not very original, but the slides were good.

'After the lecture there were the usual questions. Miss Spratt brought in the coffee and the members chatted. I was taking down my equipment and carrying it out to the car. When I'd got it out, I went straight home. My wife doesn't like my staying out too late.'

'Did you notice Major Forbes at the meeting?' asked the Inspector.

'Oh yes, he was certainly there. I remember he asked a question. Couldn't make head or tale of it myself. I'm a biologist really,' he added, apologetically. 'The Major was still there when I left. He was talking to Doolittle-Smythe. He's the Treasurer of the Society.'

'You didn't notice any unusual occurrence, or odd behaviour at the meeting?' asked the Inspector.

'Not at the BAAAS. Never!' replied Mr Bugg, firmly.

'Thank you very much for your help. Just one thing,' said the Inspector. 'We'll be sending someone round with a statement for you to sign later. Could you tell us, please whether you went out again that night, after returning home?'

The Curator showed them to the door. 'Nothing would have persuaded me to go out again,' he said.

'That was a bit of luck. I think things must be going my way at last,' said the Inspector. 'First that schoolmaster fellow turns out to be two of the people we want to see, then the Museum produces another two witnesses straight away. Not that they were witnesses of anything, though,' he added, less happily.

'They confirm the other witnesses,' Peter replied. 'Nothing happened at that meeting of the BAAAS. It never does. Yet we don't have any lead at all otherwise.'

'We've got the door-to-door men out now all round Cold Beech, to see if anyone noticed anything. Not much chance there, either,' said the Inspector.

All this time they had been walking down the main shopping street of the town. Ken turned in through the doors beside the impressive portal of the leading bank in the area, and they walked up the stairs to the first floor. He pressed a button beside a fluted glass screen, labelled 'Doolittle-Smythe and Jones. Enquiries'. Part of the screen slid back, and a very young girl, very nervous, asked,

'Can I help you?'

'I should like to see Mr Doolittle-Smythe, please,' said the Inspector.

'Have you an appointment, sir?'

'No, but it's important that I see him now. My name is Harris, Detective Inspector Harris.'

The screen slid swiftly shut. In a couple of minutes the girl reappeared on their side of it, and asked them to follow her down the corridor. She showed them into a neat office, with one wall covered by a large bookcase. A straight-backed, grey-haired gentleman, in an immaculate dark grey suit, rose from behind the desk, and extended his hand which they both shook.

'How can I help you, gentlemen?' asked Mr Doolittle-Smythe.

'We are investigating the murder of Major Forbes,' said the Inspector.

The lawyer raised his eyebrows in surprise at such immoderate language.

'Are you certain of your facts, Inspector? I understood that the gentleman concerned had fallen down a well. Is there some evidence that he didn't do this by accident?'

'We have good reasons, which I would rather not go into, for believing that the death was not an accident, sir. I wonder if you could tell us anything, or rather, everything, that happened at the meeting of the BAAAS on Saturday night. We are hoping that some little detail will give us a clue to how the Major died.'

The lawyer moved a chair from a corner, so that there were two easy chairs in front of his desk. He sat down himself, and indicated that they were to make themselves comfortable.

'I am not used to being asked to give evidence myself,' he

began, 'so this ought to be an interesting experience.' He put his elbows on the desk, and his fingertips together. His eyes fixed themselves on the ceiling over the Inspector's head. 'I arrived at the time the meeting was supposed to start. There were a few people already there, mostly sitting alone. Except the Bishop, with two clergymen. They always sit together. The rectors of Letchbury and St. Peter's Broadchester, they are.

'I went straight over to speak to Mr Bugg, the Museum curator. He does the magic lantern, you know. We had a talk about the price of replacement bulbs for his apparatus. I'm the Treasurer of the Society and have to keep account of such things. While we were talking, the hall filled. It's only a small room actually—I suppose there must have been twenty of us present.'

'Sixteen, according to the book,' corrected the Inspector.

'Sixteen. Quite a good turnout! As I was saying, everyone came in as we were chatting. The speaker came in with those nice Scottish people, the Duguids. I left him telling Mr Bugg how he wanted the slides arranged and sat down on my own. Major Forbes sat next to me just before Lady Forster introduced the speaker.

'The talk was about Roman Broadshire, by Professor Charleston. You don't want me to try to remember the text of that I hope?'

'No thank you,' put in the Inspector hurriedly. 'Let's go straight on to the questions. Was there anything unusual there?'

'Not really. What usually happens is that people either want to display their superior knowledge, or aren't ashamed to show their ignorance. Mostly the latter. Mr Hanbury, the schoolmaster, asked something that wasn't really a question, to let everyone know that he had been to Pompeii for his holidays, I remember. Forbes asked a question too. Something about the work that the Professor had done at Water End, and the Roman roads in the area. I seem to remember that he seemed pretty excited about it, but the speaker was very brusque and cut him off.'

There was a knock at the door and the girl appeared, carrying a tray with fine china cups and a large silver teapot, which she put on the desk. There was a short hiatus while tea was poured to their satisfaction. The girl retired.

'Where was I?' asked the solicitor. 'Ah—after the questions, we had a vote of thanks. Petchy, architect fellow, has an office round the corner, proposed it. Then coffee. We all circulate and talk. I suppose I had a word with nearly everyone. I would have liked to have spoken to the speaker, and paid him his expenses, but by the time I got round to it, Forbes was deep in conversation with him. I shall have to write to the Professor now, I suppose. Anyway, I had to leave. I was nearly the last to go. Mr Jones was still there, with a guest, and Mr and Mrs Duguid. I went straight home to bed. I live alone.'

'Thank you very much,' said the Inspector, with obvious sincerity, 'for such a concise and accurate account. We will be asking you to sign a statement in due course. Can you think of any other detail that might help us. How did the Major seem to you, for example? Was he his usual self?'

'Oh, I forgot that. He seemed excited, as though he was on the verge of some great discovery. He came and asked me how much we had in the excavation fund. He said he had a research dig that he wanted to do. He wouldn't give any more information, he said, till he'd got it all set up. Now I suppose I shall never know.'

The investigators thanked the lawyer once again, and showed themselves out of the office.

'Now for a quick dash over to Petchy's place, before it closes,' said the Inspector. 'We can't waste much more time on all this gossip. It's not getting us anywhere.'

The offices of C A Petchy, ARIBA, F Inst TP, etc were only a short walk from the lawyer's office. They were in a building which appeared from the outside to be a row of whitewashed cottages, with a large slate nameplate beside one of the doors. Inside was a different matter. It was a sparsely furnished 'contemporary' open-plan office suite, all oiled teak, coir matting, Anglepoise lamps and rubber-tree plants. Mr Petchy, who looked rather like Oscar Wilde as seen by Aubrey Beardsley in his worst moments, saw them in his office, which was a partitioned corner of a large drawing office on the first floor.

'My dear Inspector, how can I possibly be of assistance to the long arm of the law?' he effused, extending a limp hand, more as if he expected it to be kissed than shaken.

The Inspector explained the nature of their enquiry and asked Mr Petchy the same question that he had already asked so many times.

'Ah! Yes! One must be certain of such details in a case of this sort must one not? Now, let me see—I worked late here at the office. One has one's own provisions here, you know.'

'One does?' echoed the Inspector, outrageously.

'Oh yes! One does indeed. One must have an office with every, but every convenience,' the architect gushed on, undeterred. 'I went straight over to the meeting from here. One has to appear on time if one is to be noticed. I had a book with me and I sat in the front row of chairs and read it until the meeting started. Frightfully good talk—Romans in Broadshire—ever such fun! First time I'd seen that lovely dig of Charleston's on the screen. Such precision! Made old Forbes mad at times. I used to do the site plans for Forbes you know. He was always jealous of Charleston. He always used to say that it wasn't right that that dreadful man should come into his county with more money that he had, and all that labour, either paid or poor students who had to do what they were told. All he had was a lot of old women, most of the time; couldn't afford to pay them, and couldn't order them about in case they ran away. No wonder Charleston's excavations always looked so good. Not that Forbes' work wasn't of a very high standard.

'After the lecture there were those utterly dreary questions from the floor. Mostly ignorant sorts of things. Except old Forbes. He asked Charleston whether he had considered the possibility that the Water End site might have been a Roman station on the Itinerary. I don't believe that Charleston had given the matter a moment's thought before, but he's a lovely man, and thinks so quickly on his feet. He must have so many facts at his command. He recited the relevant bit of the Itinerary off by heart, with all the names and distances, and pointed out that the Major's question had already been asked before by the father of County History, Chipperfield, in the early nineteenth century. What he was implying, of course, was that Forbes was out of date, and tarred with the same brush as the dear old antiquaries of centuries ago. Rather unfair on the dear old boy.'

'Thank you, sir,' said the Inspector, rather surprised at the directness of the information he had been given. 'What happened after the questions?'

The architect struck a pose of concentration that might have served as a model for Rodin.

'Coffee,' he said. 'Lovely sweet, black coffee. And the old peripatetic bit. All wandering around. No! I lie, Inspector. A beautifully elegantly constructed vote of thanks was proposed to the learned speaker. I cannot tell a lie, I did it with my little tongue in my cheek. Buttered him up like anything. He loved it. *Then* the coffee and the walk-around. Talk to everyone that matters, that's what one must do. I don't expect that much of it sticks, but one must keep the face in the public mind. I remember Broad, Bugg, those Duguids, a genuine bishop, with attendant deities, a brief chat with the Prof, Lady Forster, Jones the Museum, and, of course, Forbes.'

'Was there anything unusual about his manner?' asked the Inspector.

'Oh! The dear old thing didn't have any presentiment or

premonition of doom, or anything like that. He seemed all set for his next excavation. Wanted me to arrange time off to come along with my little tape measure and all that. Very excited by the prospect, he was.'

'Where was he going to dig next?' Peter asked.

'He always had to have his little secrets. He said he'd let me know when he'd got it all ready. One has to arrange permission from landowners, finance, and all that kind of thing. But he really was dead keen on it. Wanted to start next April.'

'One last thing, sir,' said the Inspector. 'I shall have to ask you to sign a statement containing a brief outline of what happened that night. Could you tell us when you left, and what you did after the meeting?'

'Oh, I never did it, Inspector, cross my heart,' the architect burst out, looking frightened. 'I left fairly late. Forbes was talking to Prof Charleston. Everyone else had either left, or was on the doorstep with their coats on. A beautifully uniformed man with a bunch of keys was waiting to lock up. The Duguids were waiting at the bottom of the steps to pounce on the speaker. Dreadful people, absolute snobs; never work on a dig unless the director has a first class degree from Cambridge, and is a fellow of the Society of Antiquaries. Spend their summer holidays that way, and then have winter ones on cultural cruises of the Mediterranean with the big names, and sit at the captain's table. But nauseating!'

'What did you do after you left?' the Inspector broke in.

'I just went home to bye-byes. I share a flat, you can always check up on me,' said the architect.

'I hope that won't be necessary. Thank you for your help.'

CHAPTER 13

The Lady President

'With any luck we can finish the interviews that fall to our lot by teatime,' the policeman gloated, as they left the architect's bijou office. 'Just three more of them to see: Her Ladyship the President of the BAAAS, and the two Scots. What was the name?'

'Duguid,' Peter answered. 'I don't see quite what you're feeling so pleased about. The leg work may be nearly done, but you seem to have found out precisely nothing of any use.'

'Pessimist!' replied the Inspector. 'The case is going to be solved by the routine enquiries going on elsewhere. All we are finding out is the background of the picture. There is always the happy bit of serendipity, like the murder weapon being found under our very eyes. You never know. Something may turn up!'

They walked back to the car and made themselves comfortable for the ride out to Stowden Old Hall, which Peter insisted on calling 'the Presidential address', because it was the home of the Lady President of the County Archaeological Society, Lady Forster. As they drove out into the countryside again, into the setting sun, Peter explained the position of the Lady in the hierarchy.

'County, very definitely,' he said, 'of the first water. Every inch "Your Ladyship" at home and out of it. There is actually a Lord Forster too, but he doesn't come into the picture at all. Lives in Essex somewhere. I think they are officially divorced. She lives by her pen—she is Elizabeth Forest, the historical novelist, you know. Improbable but very romantic stuff set mainly in the Regency period. Utter rubbish, but a goldmine. She seems to share her lot with a gentleman called Colonel Stevens, who is euphemistically referred to as her agent.'

'I see,' the Inspector replied, with a grimace. 'She is like the Lord Lieutenant, the Bishop, and Caesar's wife. She really ought to be outside my terms of reference. The Lord Lieutenant and the clergy at the meeting have been asked to make brief written statements by the Chief Constable himself, no less. Saves work for the copper, I suppose. Pity he didn't think to ask her Ladyship as well.'

'Perhaps he thought the experience would do you a power of good, old son,' teased Peter. 'After all, you must learn sometime to move in the best circles.'

'I prefer to go straight. Anyway, what's so special about her? Has she really got an aristocratic background, or did she marry one?'

'I've never thought to ask. One doesn't somehow. She's really the County *par excellence*.'

Soon they turned in through the gateway of Stowden Old Hall, flanked by tall brick piers with stags at bay against the evening sky. The drive took them in a curve through neglected shrubberies, to disclose a surprise vista of the house front at a distance of about a quarter of a mile. It was a red brick building, very square and solid, dating from the beginning of the eighteenth century. Close to the house the gardens were well cared for, and the lawns trimmed. The lateness of the season had permitted the last of the dahlias to provide a colourful and unexpected foreground for the Michaelmas daisies. The car pulled up outside the doorway flanked by ionic columns and surmounted by a pediment containing a carved stone coat of arms of considerable complication and quartering. The Inspector pulled a wrought iron handle which connected to a crank which disappeared through a slot in the stonework surrounding the door jamb.

They waited for some minutes in silence. The archaeologist examined the doorway for any sign of a hidden electrical bell push, and raised his hand to knock on the door, which was immediately opened from inside by a stocky, middle-aged woman, wearing a blue nylon overall. She had a short cigarette end hanging miraculously from her lower lip. She spoke.

'Yerse?'

'I am Detective Inspector Harris, of the Broadshire Constabulary. I wonder it I might have a word with her Ladyship?' He handed the woman a card.

The woman peered at the card, drawing her head back and half closing her eyes against the trickle of tobacco smoke that wound its way up her left cheek. Then she turned the card over, and repeated the performance. Then she turned and walked away, without a word.

A very loud and affected voice was raised somewhere at a distance inside the house. In the quiet of the estate, the words could be heard quite distinctly, becoming louder as the speaker approached the door.

'A detective, did you say, my dear woman. But how perfectly charming for us all. We must invite him in for just a teeny-weeny drink, even if he is on duty. Perhaps he's collecting for a police charity or something.'

The owner of the voice appeared before them. She was tall, and clad in a neat tweed suit. At first, in the half light of the hall, Peter thought that she might be quite young. As he was introduced, and went into the house, his eyes became accustomed to the light and he realised his mistake. The face which he saw was a masterpiece of cosmetic art, but nevertheless, a mask, covering a face that could no longer even be called middle-aged. He further realised that the lady was, to put it mildly, a little the worse for drink.

'Do come in, my dear Inspector. I am most charmed to meet you and your charming assistant,' she gushed, steering them into a large drawing room, panelled with light oak, and furnished with enormous and overstuffed furniture. 'Please sit down and tell me what it's all about.'

98

As they tried to sink gracefully into the chairs—they had the most peculiar proportions, the seat being only just over a foot from the floor, but nearly three feet from front to back—her ladyship rang a bell and asked the woman who had opened the door to them, who somehow still had the same length of cigarette, still alight, adhering to her lip, to bring in the drink trolley.

The Inspector began by explaining the nature of their enquiries, and trying, as before, to get the background to Major Forbes' last public appearance. Unfortunately, at this juncture the door was bumped open and the drink trolley appeared, a three-tiered thing in rosewood and gilt, with large cartwheels with gold spokes. Pushing it was a rather stiff looking man, of definitely military bearing. His hair was grey, but cut very short-back-and-sides. His face was flushed with many campaigns with the bottle. He had a short trimmed moustache, and protruding blue eyes. He wore a guards' tie, a smart blue suit and highly-polished light-brown boots.

'Have you heard?' her ladyship bellowed. 'They've gone and murdered poor old Booboo Forbes.'

'Couldn't stand the man myself. Always pryin' into me military background. Always tryin' to find if we had served in any stations together. Don't think he believed half of what I told him.'

No more would I, thought Peter to himself. This fellow is too like the cartoon caricature of a confidence man impersonating an officer and a gentleman to be true!

'Good evening, Colonel,' said the Inspector, relying on his memory and trusting to luck. Lady Forster apologised and introduced her agent. Drinks were poured, and the Inspector again steered the conversation back to the subject of their enquiries.

'Oh! Those wretched Antiques, they're more trouble than they are worth to me, dear Inspector,' her ladyship effused. 'I'm a sort of figure-head really, you know. They go on so about brasses and heraldry and all that sort of technical stuff. All too awfully abstract for me. And this last thing was all about the Romans. There's nothing human about the Romans; been dead too long. My period is far more romantic. And profitable,' she added in a frank afterthought. 'Let's see. I drove myself to the meeting and arrived quite late. Nearly everyone was there. I went straight up to the platform, where I was joined by the speaker. I had met him before, when he was digging at Water End. We were able to have a few brief words before I introduced him.

'It was an interesting lecture, I imagine, for those who enjoy that sort of thing. A few of the old dears asked questions afterwards. The dear Major was one of them, now I come to think of it. Luckily they didn't expect me to repeat the questions back; the speaker answered direct. I really wouldn't know what they were on about. I made my exit as soon as I decently could, without appearing rude. The speaker was soon in conversation with the members over coffee and I slipped out.'

'Did you notice anything about the Major that evening?' asked the Inspector.

'He didn't have a crimson aura or anything, if that's what you mean,' Lady Forster answered flippantly, fluttering her eyelashes in what she evidently thought was a girlish manner. 'No, seriously, he seemed in very high spirits.'

'Could you tell us anything about him? We have found it difficult to find anyone who knew him well, and who might be able to help us.'

'I can't claim to know the old darling all that well myself. He was a charming old thing. A proper gentleman. I imagine he had served in India. He didn't seem to have any family that I knew of. Lived by himself. Wrote books. Directed excavations. Used to drink and smoke a little. Seemed to have got a little old for the other thing, don't you know.'

'You can't think of any reason why anyone should want

to have him dead?' the Inspector added, directly, rising and putting his empty glass on the drink trolley.

'Dear me, no! He could be a bit of a tartar on the dig, and I can imagine him being a bit pigheaded over some idea. But I can't imagine anyone I know of wanting to do more than punch him on the nose, if that.'

The Inspector and the archaeologist managed to excuse themselves on the grounds of duty, and refused further offers of drinks. As they sped off down the drive, Peter glanced back and saw the Lady President and her agent standing on the front step of the house, with full glasses in their hands.

'Two more to go,' said the Inspector, with relief. 'The Duguids. What do we know already about them?'

'Doolittle-Smythe described them as "charming",' answered Peter.

'That architect type, Petchy, described them as "dreadful people, absolute snobs ... but nauseating",' replied the Inspector, showing off his talent for remembering conversation. 'So what we expect now is to meet a couple of charming creepers. I wonder if they can tell us anything. They were reported to us as hanging about after the meeting.'

CHAPTER 14

The Duguids

The Duguids lived in a large half-timbered building in a wooded area that had somehow become a dispersed estate for 'executives'. It was the only genuine old building in a scattered group of stockbroker Tudor. Like its near neighbours, two hundred yards away through the woods, it had a garage large enough to house the two cars necessary for the existence of the inhabitants. The estate was at least two miles from the nearest town and station; while husband was commuting, wife must have a car for the shopping. The house itself was entirely spoiled by the fact that the infilling between the timber frame had been rendered and given that roughcast finish known as 'Tyrolean', which had afterwards been painted the colour of mustard pickle. As they approached the house, its colour shone out in the last rays of the setting sun. The lights were on in nearly every room. The Inspector rang the doorbell.

The door was opened by a small, middle-aged lady, with very short hair. Her face was devoid of lipstick or any visible makeup, and she was wearing a grey trouser suit. The general effect, Peter thought, was of a public-school prefect who had been taking the wrong sort of hormone tablets. The Inspector introduced themselves, and they were invited inside.

The interior of the house had that curious paradoxical lack of opulence that sometimes goes with affected culture and lots of money. It appeared at first sight to be almost bare. An open plan had been achieved by judicious removal of inside walls. Furniture was at a minimum, and lighting was from stagey spotlights concealed in holes in the ceiling. Most of these lights were arranged to illuminate what were evidently intended to be works of art: objects of wire or concrete at random over the floor. The furniture was of tubular steel. The house was as comfortable a home as, say, the Hayward Gallery, and less functional.

As they walked in, a man entered from the other side of the living space. At first, under the almost vertical lighting, he looked like everyone's idea of the bright young thing: flowery shirt with open collar to display a large golden medallion on a hairy chest, rope-soled sandals and all. On closer inspection, it could be seen that this was no bright young thing. It was a tarnished old thing, dressed up. They had found the saprophytic Duguids. After introductions, Mrs Duguid who had indeed a charming manner, took charge of them. There was no doubt from her accent of her Highland origins.

'Inspector, you must have something to drink? But just a little coffee then? Black or white? Will you get it then, hubby dear? You simply must look at this; isn't it charming? Picked it up at the Lachat gallery only last week. It's called "whither mankind whither". It's by Bankowitcz. Isn't he just too wonderful for words? What was that? Oh, your enquiries. But wouldn't life be unbearable if we hadn't got time to just stand and stare just *occasionally*. Of course, you work. It must be just fascinating working with all those policemen and meeting all those real criminals. . .'

Eventually, by tactful handling and a little rearrangement of the furniture, the Inspector managed to get all four of them seated in such a position that they could see one another's faces. He then explained the purpose of their visit, and asked for an account of the BAAAS meeting. Mrs Duguid did most of the talking, with her husband occasionally adding circumstantial corroboration.

'We had dinner early that evening. We didn't want to be late for the meeting, because we were delivering the speaker,' she explained.

'Delivering the speaker? What do you mean?' asked the

Inspector.

'He came down early so that he could have dinner with us. We're old friends of his, you know. He's such a clever man. We always go and work on his dig every summer, wherever it is. He's so interesting to talk to. Well, as I was saying, we had dinner early so that we could deliver him on time. Alan—that's Professor Charleston—was going to tell us all about the Romans. We delivered him to the hall. Then we sort of lost him until after the meeting was over. It was such an interesting talk. He's an authority on the period, you know. I couldn't remember half the fascinating things he said.'

'What happened after the lecture?' prompted the Inspector.

'The usual things. Boring questions from the rest of the Society,' she answered, revealingly.

'Did Major Forbes ask a question, do you remember?' asked the Inspector, hoping to steer the account into more useful channels.

'He did too! Something about Roman roads, I think.'

'Itineraries,' put in her husband, laconically.

'That's it. Whatever those are. He asked about itinersomethings,' she went on. 'Of course, dear Alan was able to answer him. The Major is, or rather was, a very good man, but the Professor, well, he *is* a professor, isn't he? Then,' she went on, 'we had a vote of thanks, from that queer little architect person—'

'Petchy,' said Mr Duguid.

'That's right, Mr Petchy,' she continued, 'and then we had coffee. We were able to talk to the Lord Lieutenant and tell him about our visit to Malta. He's been there too. We didn't talk to many of the others; they're so standoffish. And they're only ordinary anyway. Except the Bishop. But he's an Anglican.'

Peter recognised the Duguids for what they were—the snobs spiritual and temporal always to be found on the

104

fringes of every archaeological society, preying upon the gentry and the academics and travelling widely, so that they could tell other people, the ordinary mortals, about it. He could understand how the Professor had arranged that the Duguids should 'sort of lose him', rather than be invited home for a drink and a dose of culture. What could such people contribute to society? They were unqualified entrepreneurs, collecting experiences merely to impress, not to inform. He was not surprised that the Inspector did not ask any further questions, but concentrated hard on extricating them from the flypaper of Mrs Duguid's conversation.

As they drove away from the house, Ken Harris made a statement which was a masterly summing-up of the Duguids.

'Arrested social development. They are in the same bracket, morally, as your second form at school. They have got past the sort of argument which goes "He did. No he didn't", and have arrived at the stage of "My father says so, and he ought to know because he's cleverer than yours". Only difference is that they have substituted people of rank and station for their father figures. It'd be no damn use asking them if they'd seen anything unusual that night, any more than you'd really ask your second form. You'd be swamped with unusual phenomena, from psychic auras to men in black cloaks and shovel hats carrying bombs. They are all right as corroborating what we already know, but you couldn't take them any further. Blimey! Just imagine if you had to get one of them into the witness box!'

'That's not really fair,' Peter remonstrated. 'You don't know what Mr was thinking. *She* did all the talking.'

'Yes,' agreed the Inspector, grudgingly. 'Interview him on his own before she has helped him get the facts, or what she imagines are the facts, straight, and you might get something. It isn't worth it in this instance, is it?'

CHAPTER 15

Interrogation

That evening, Peter and the Inspector worked late over a few bottles of brown ale in front of the fire in Peter's study. Ken had brought round copies of all the statements so far made, and Peter had his notes of the interviews. The Inspector was dejected.

'We have,' he said, as he helped himself to the third bottle, 'lots of what might be called facts. There is no doubt that most of what we know about this case is corroborated to a surprising degree. It seems reasonably certain that Major Frederick Forbes met his death under circumstances which preclude premeditation. Even if anyone had known of his jaunts to the Villa for ready cash, tax free, it is unlikely that they could have kept watch for him to oblige, without arousing suspicion about their own movements. The Major lived almost incommunicado for some time before the event, and we have no reason to believe that there was any threat to him before it either. All the statements about what happened that evening dovetail quite neatly, and do not suggest any reason for homicide. Of course, if there is any motive like blackmail, or threatened blackmail, we would find it hard to discover.

'Suppose, for instance, that he had found out that Doolittle-Smythe had been cooking the books—or indeed that any one of the people he spoke to on that evening had been guilty of some misconduct. He would only have needed to have a quiet word with him, without the others knowing.'

'That's all very well as a theory,' suggested Peter, 'but where is any trace of corroborative evidence? His bank account is blameless, so we have no history of blackmail, and he didn't, to our knowledge, receive any information which he could have used for blackmail—or, being more charitable, have threatened to expose unless matters were put right. Actually, everyone seemed to admire his integrity, so that would be more in keeping. But we have no facts to suggest it.'

'True,' agreed the Inspector, 'but have you any better suggestion?'

'Not at present,' said Peter, 'so let's get back to the facts, as you call them, rather than the conjecture. We've looked at all the statements, including the ones from the clergymen and the Professor. There is nothing inconsistent in any of them, and fundamentally they all tell the same boring story of what doesn't happen at an archaeological society meeting. We are unable to find any salient point requiring amplification. We have statements from all the people who saw the Major that night. In fact,' he went on, 'the only fact which seems to be uncorroborated is the fact of homicide. Your police doctor, I notice, neither confirms nor denies carbon dioxide as the possible cause of death.'

'What he actually said,' the Inspector explained, 'when we talked this evening, was that he rather liked the idea of carbon dioxide being the instrument or just cause of the death, although the actual shuffling off of the mortal coil, the terminal phase as it were, was drowning. His lungs filled with water. Very bad for breathing, you know. Lots of carbon dioxide in the blood could have been because the heart had stopped and various metabolic processes had gone on anyway.'

'So we deduce murder by fire extinguisher because we want to. The extinguisher could be empty from a number of causes, including simple vandalism.'

'Not so really.' The Inspector poured another drink. 'There must have been some odd goings on at the Villa that night. We have to explain the absence of the ladder from the well, and the door wedged open. It all fits, you know.'

'In which case,' Peter agreed, 'we must look for someone

107

else to fit the bill of the-last-person-to-see-the-deceased-alive. And all your enquiries have so far led to no-one. No motive, no opportunity. In fact, as far as I can see, even if you were to produce your murderer red-handed, covered with paint from the fire extinguisher, you would have a job convincing a jury that murder had been done. Can you imagine a defence counsel making hay with our theory? Counsel to expert medical witness: "Is it not possible that the deceased could have fallen where he was found, without any obvious bruising?" And counsel to fire officer: "Is it not possible that the extinguisher that you were about to replace without comment might have come to be exhausted from some innocent cause? Have you any experience of such an instrument being used as a murder weapon?" '

'I think,' said the Inspector, folding his arms and looking very serious, 'that it's time you came clean. I'm not sure that I ought not to caution you, before you begin.'

'Whatever have I done now?' asked Peter, somewhat taken aback.

'That remains to be seen, but I assure you that you needn't expect to get away with it, whatever it was. It's about time you answered a few questions yourself. However,' he went on, apparently relenting a little, 'I should be glad if you'd broach another bottle before the interrogation begins.' Peter obliged.

'I am not as slow as you seem to think,' the Inspector continued. 'On the morning Black discovered the body, I asked you to come along as an expert witness. It seemed to me, at the time, that the problem might appeal to you as being an odd association of objects if nothing else, and that your knowledge of local archaeologists might come in useful. So far my judgement has been well founded, and you have acted out your part as Virgil in this Divine Comedy. You have, however, made two slips which I find highly suspicious. Do you remember what you said when I asked you if you knew the well at Cold Beech Villa? I'll tell you what you said,' he went on without waiting for a reply. 'You said, "I dug it a long time ago" or words to that effect. This morning, you took me over to the site and displayed considerable knowledge of local geography. You even regaled me with stories about the excavation of the Villa. Since you apparently had something to do with the digging, which Black told us was directed by Forbes himself, it follows that you too knew Forbes. You've let me spend a lot of time asking people their opinions of the Major, without once offering any opinion yourself. Explain yourself.'

'I don't think I can explain myself,' Peter retorted. 'I thought you knew of my connection with Cold Beech. You wanted other people's opinions more to find out about them than to find out about him, surely. Anyway, apart from occasionally meeting him at a conference or something, and buying him a drink, I haven't had anything to do with him since the dig, over twenty years ago. I was only a schoolboy at the time, too.'

'Don't get all steamy about it, Peter,' said the Inspector, in a rather ironic attempt to mollify the archaeologist. 'I was only kidding. Anyway, I have checked up on you, and it seems that you had at least three witnesses to the fact that you were sticking broken pottery together at the time the Major died.'

'You unprincipled thing! Do you mean to say that I have been riding with the hounds and running with the fox all day?'

'No-one is completely free from suspicion, old lad. I've been wasting lots of man hours on lots of people. Including you,' admitted the Inspector. 'Now, free from all suspicion of the crime, tell me everything you know, or think you know, about the Major.'

'Don't forget I never knew him well,' Peter began.

'As good a place to start with,' said the Inspector. 'Why was that? You'd known him twenty years by your own admission.'

'The main factors, as far as I am concerned,' said Peter, 'are two almost unbridgeable gaps. The first was the generation gap; he was older than my own father. The second was the social gap; he was one of *them*, and I wasn't. I am a grammar school scholarship boy, not born into the gentry, you know. I imagine that when we began work on the Villa, this didn't show. I was a polite lad,—once. I admired him enormously for his ability as an archaeologist, and as an organiser, but even as a schoolboy, or perhaps I should say *because* I was an adolescent schoolboy, I discovered his imperfections, his feet of clay. The main one, in my eyes at the time, was his habit of playing to the gallery. Given the slightest excuse, he would take an object from one of the younger diggers and stand in silence examining it through a watchmaker's eyeglass, before declaiming upon its archaeological importance. It made the young digger feel quite important, but I noticed that he only did it when there was a large audience, of either inexperienced diggers or the general public, to witness the display of erudition. Then I noticed how often it happened that important discoveries were left in the ground, all cleaned up for the camera, until an important visitor (county or academic) was present to see it removed.

'Faced by the overtly refined, my reaction then, as now, is to become obviously corblimey myself and my disinclination to work for effect led to quite a lot of friction between director and supervisor, as I then was. Sometimes, when he had a bit of a hangover, he would refuse to speak to me. I found that this made very little difference to the work that was done on my part of the site, and gave me much more confidence for when I eventually came to direct my own excavations. Oh yes, he used to drink quite a lot, and the number of young ladies who used to go home with him to see the collection of coins he kept at home for safety was enough to make an adolescent green with envy. There was a

110

lot to admire about him, from a schoolboy's point of view.

'I think that the old boy finally gave me up as being beyond redemption when I left school, went to a redbrick university, got a degree in chemistry and did my national service in the ranks—not even the army ranks. The only thing we had in common was our interest in archaeology, and the remnants of that *esprit de corps* which comes from pioneering on a rather spectacular site. We remained acquaintances, rather than friends.'

'Sounds a pretty ambivalent relationship to me. All set for the Oedipus touch. What you have just said, coupled with your special knowledge of chemistry and the properties of carbon dioxide could make you into a first class suspect. If you hadn't got an alibi,' added the Inspector, 'and if this story wasn't so old. And, come to think of it, you'd need more of a motive than your disillusionment over the imperfections of a schoolboy hero. Perhaps you'd better quickly recapitulate on what we know about the deceased as a person.'

'Really, you know, I think the evidence given by many of our witnesses has given us a good picture. Typical military man of the old school, accurate to the last detail. A bit of a showman, because that is the way to succeed if you are running things for the county set. "Fierce and friendly" I think Bill called him. Describes him to a "t". Like my old station adjutant, all smiles one minute, jump on you with both feet the next. It is impossible to imagine him getting mixed up in any shady business. He would never become a blackmailer, and woe betide anyone who might try to put the screws on him. He might have been exasperating, and, I am sure, a bit of a Hector in his latter days, but you could take him or leave him. If you didn't want to salute and say "yessir" you could always do what I did, and go away. He'll be a great loss, if only because there will be no-one firm enough to steer the BAAAS in the path of righteousness. To put it more firmly: I can think of no good reason for anyone

111

wanting to kill the Major. Nor do I think you could produce enough evidence to convince the unconverted that he really was murdered.'

'I take your point,' said the Inspector. 'Where do we go from here? The Coroner wants satisfying. What am I to do now? I can't really even justify the enquiries that we have made. Suggestion?'

Peter stared into the fire for a while.

'I still think that it must be murder. We can't prove it. We can go on trying, of course. Do you know the Coroner? It looks as though you'll have to take the coward's way out. Produce the minimum of evidence and ask for an adjournment *sine die*. Or, if he, or your superiors won't hear of that, produce enough evidence to convince the jury that an open verdict is in order. That is an admission of defeat, but would allow your enquiries to go on.'

'I'll start getting things in motion with the Coroner's officer at Broadchester along those lines, just to see if the Coroner will wear it. That should give us another couple of days to go on stirring. There is still one thing that we should check up on, you know. All the stories do dovetail quite closely, and they all point to one man who was the last person known to see the Major alive. On principle, I think we should check on him more closely than before. It seems to me that as the hall emptied after the meeting, Forbes and the speaker, Professor Charleston, were sort of left behind deep in conversation.'

'With the Duguids couching at the door, waiting for the Prof to emerge so that they could pounce on him again. They say they lost him after the meeting. I suppose he must have slipped out the back way in order to avoid getting entangled further at that time of night. I can't say I blame him,' said Peter, pulling a face.

'Ah! So if we wish to know what really happened, just to sort out those dying moments of the meeting, we shall have to ask our two sychophantic Scots.' The Inspector paused, rubbing his forehead in a tired bothered gesture. Then his face brightened. 'On second thoughts,' he said, brightly, 'what we'll do is interview Mr Duguid on his own. First thing tomorrow I'll get my sergeant to phone his home and find out where he works. The lads will have to get statements properly signed and all that from them anyway. We can use that as an excuse.'

CHAPTER 16

Mr Duguid's story

Mr Duguid, they learned the following morning, worked in an industrial estate at Letchbury. The address was given as Tull and MacInthrop, Watt Avenue. They set off to drive down at about nine am. The weather was still mellow.

'I don't like Letchbury one bit,' said Peter, as they set out. 'It's got no character at all. When the electric lamp people started up there just before the beginning of this century, there was practically nothing there, except a small village with village green, duck pond and stocks. The railway was close, and it wasn't too far from the main road. Even the canal was thriving. It was a stroke of genius to see that the means of transport were all there, just waiting to be spurred off. And then, of course, the choice of industry was a masterpiece. Just when all the electricity generating companies came into being, there was a firm all tooled up and raring to go. It meant expansion in a big way for the town, and death to the village.'

'They built to last in those days, old son,' observed the Inspector, as they turned into the main road and set off southwards.

'They also put the gasometers next to the church. On a Sunday morning, before the dinners are cooked, you can stand on the top of a gasometer and look down on the flag flying from the church tower,' retorted Peter. 'What's the good of building to last if you build such monstrous buildings? They loved all that yellow and red brickwork, gothic arches, fretted ridgetiles and dragon finials against the sky.'

'All I can say is, it's a pity we don't take a bit more pride in appearance nowadays. It wouldn't hurt us to decorate things a bit. Look at that little lot,' Ken waved his hand towards a row of council houses. 'Sort of thing I used to make out of shoe boxes when I was a nipper. Absolutely devoid of any decoration at all. Modern houses are all right, providing you are inside looking out, not outside trying to admire the view.'

'Trouble is,' observed Peter, after a long silence, 'we all tend to worship accuracy nowadays. You probably think when I go all gaga over some old building that it's just sentiment, and that the whole thing is romantic because it's warped and twisted. This isn't really true, you know; nowadays everything is standardised. In the old days, when you wanted to build a cottage, you cut down a few trees, and in all likelihood, instead of sawing timber you split it with wedges and then dressed it with adzes and side axes, making everything slightly warped, but very strong because your beams followed along their own grain. Today, timber is expensive, and you can't afford to overdesign. If the standard says you use timber which is four by two, then you get it exactly that size, cut automatically and exactly straight. That reminds me. I once heard a workman say, when he was handed the plans of a roof carcase, "What's all this then? I've always used four-be-two. No-one's ever told me to use four-be-four before".'

'You are just objecting to progress,' chipped in the Inspector. 'I bet the Iron Age people thought the Roman architects were a load of squares. Look at their art, and the few huts you archaeologists have managed to find which belong to the pre-Roman Iron Age. I bet the average Belgic tribesman didn't know what a straight line was.'

'I think I'd rather have been Belgic, you know. Trouble is, accuracy or pseudo-accuracy seems to slip into everything nowadays. If it can be measured, we measure it and record it. We may not know what to do with it, but we record it all the same. Archaeological reports are slowly becoming more and more infested with figures—figures which, I might point out, are meaningless to most of the archaeologists themselves. I came across a pathologist's report that gave the average age of twenty Roman skeletons to two decimal places. That is, to one part in two thousand, based on figures which were themselves guesses anyway. I bet you don't know your *own* age to the nearest thousandth!'

'We all know,' said the Inspector, 'in the Force, that you can teach people simple arithmetic with difficulty, but you cannot teach them common sense by any known process.'

'I'll give you an example of the sort of thing we all subscribe to without thinking in archaeology. We can measure distances with considerable accuracy so, of course, we do just that. Everything we find tends to get "measured in" to a trench. By reproducing the dimensions recorded, the objects could be put back in their original positions when the trench was filled in. We all have sitebooks full of measurements which eventually have to be ditched. It is, of course, the relative positions of things that really matter. You know the sort of thing from your own work: "Was the piece of paper on or under the corpse?" is a meaningful question in terms of chronology.'

'I see what you mean. We do the same sort of thing with road accidents, you know. Before the vehicles are moved in the case of a serious accident, their positions are marked and our uniformed laddies, with their fluorescent coats, risk life and limb to measure the road and mark on the vehicles. It is a useful reminder, of course, when used with sense. I remember one of my people having to phone up a man who was involved in a nasty smash at Durford, to ask him which way he was travelling. Forgotten to mark the front of the car on his plan. The driver said he couldn't help, as the car might have been spun round by the impact anyway. And then the chief asked me whether we had enough to make a charge of dangerous driving!'

'I think my most irritating case was when I did a dig for a certain museum curator, who shall be nameless. We dug a trench about twenty feet long and four wide in the very middle of a forty acre field. He insisted that we put in pegs to facilitate measurement. We found six sherds of soggy pottery in that trench. They were all accurately measured into the plan. Then the twit insisted that the exact position of the trench to the nearest three inches was not only a desirable datum—it was absolutely essential. It took a professional surveyor a morning's work (for which he was paid) to mark in the trench on a plan. The whole site was then completely removed by a gravel pit. The map was so large that the blockmaker had to reduce it to about a twentieth of its original area for publication, and the trench which had utilised all that skill and expertise looked like a flydirt. Still, as the curator said, the principle was maintained. If you want to locate the original positions of a few sherds of pottery in a non-existent trench in a field that had disappeared, just consult the records in his attic.'

'Sounds like one of those old service sayings,' said the Inspector. 'If it's going to move, measure it!'

'When some of Professor Charleston's students die, you'll find three dimensional recording engraved upon their hearts. If you can't be inspired, be accurate. Not a bad motto for an archaeologist.'

'Do you think it's got anything to offer the detective? Ah! I think we turn off here for the industrial estate.'

The car turned off the main road down a new concrete road, flanked at the entrance by very new looking boards, declaiming that they had reached Lethwick Manor Estate, and containing the names of all the firms occupying premises on the site. They were inserted on long strips, like the arrivals and departures board at a railway station.

The owners of the estate were very conscious of their responsibility in an age when ordinary people were becoming more and more aware of the impact on their environment caused by industry. The road had wide verges of well trimmed grass, with standard trees planted in it. The fronts of the factories, which were all single-storied buildings, were designed to blend with their neighbours, and each had its own flower beds and shrubberies.

'Pretty, isn't it?' asked the Inspector. 'It's all a false front really. I was called in a little while ago to investigate a theft from a lead mill along here. All these sites back straight onto fields, with a long drop down because they levelled the site when they built. It's left to the individual firms to fence the property, so security is a nightmare. And of course, most of their waste gets tipped over the edge to pollute the land.' He slowed down. 'Ask this lad here the way to Watt Avenue.'

The lad indicated, a long-haired youth in a brown boiler suit, was not very coherent, but they managed in the end to find that Watt Avenue was a turning off Newcomen Way, just before Joule Drive.

'They ought to expand this and realise the potential of the street names,' suggested Peter. 'How about "Chain Drive"?'

'I should like to open a locomotive works at "Permanent Way".'

They located the works of Messrs Tull and MacInthrop. It looked like any other building, apart from the firm's name in large letters over the front. There was no indication what the inhabitants did for a living. Whatever it was, it could provide Duguid with that large house, furnished with works of modern art, and still give him enough over to run two cars and take holidays in the Mediterranean.

Inside the front door of the building, they were straight into what was jokingly called 'Reception'. There was no-one there to receive them. Peter walked around the room, which was large with windows looking out into the road. The floor was tiled in bright black and white thermoplastic tiles. The furniture consisted of a dozen armchairs, a similar number of ashtrays on tall stands and three coffee tables with magazines on them. Peter glanced at the literature. It was concerned with general science, engineering and chemical engineering.

'They say it pays to advertise,' he remarked to the Inspector. 'I wonder what these people make.'

A door opened to admit a young lady that Peter was sure he wouldn't have looked at on the street.

'Can I 'elp you?' she asked.

'My name is Harris, Detective Inspector Harris. We'd like to have a word with Mr Duguid, if it is convenient.'

The girl said, 'Oooh!' and retreated. They never saw her again.

The next person to come through the door was Mr Duguid himself. He was no longer the person they had met at home. His clothes were now conventional to the ultimate degree. White shirt, regimental tie, knot just the right size, dark blue suit by a very good tailor indeed. Gold cufflinks and watch. Rotary Club badge in lapel buttonhole. Shining morning face. And actually speaking in complete sentences!

'Ah! Pleased to meet you again, my dear Inspector. I somehow expected that you would come over to see me sometime today,' said the Scot, rolling his r's with deliberation. 'You'll be wanting to know what happened after the meeting last Saturday, so you've come to me in my more formal habitat. It's difficult to get what you want from a man when he's in his home environment. Especially when his wife is there to correct him or prompt him,' he added, revealingly. 'Come through into my office.'

It was clear that the office was part of an area which was separated from the actual physical business of the works by fibreboard partitions. The light was entirely artificial. A typewriter could be heard clattering away behind one wall, and a loud telephone conversation of which the phrasing not the actual wording could be discerned, was taking place behind the opposite wall. The other pair of walls concealed a corridor down which people passed at intervals in loud conversation, and the mysterious work of Tull and

MacInthrop hammering, hissing and clanging.

As they sat themselves down in front of Duguid's desk, which was a modest affair groaning under the weight of papers and magazines, Peter looked around him. Personal filing cabinet; bookcase—technical books; stand with bowler hat and umbrella. On the walls: progress chart, metric conversion table and centre-spread nude from Playboy magazine, neatly and professionally framed.

Duguid offered them cigars. Peter accepted one and lit up.

'I was thinking on the way to work this morning,' said Duguid, 'that you would be coming back to me, or to both of us, to ask us an obvious question which must have been bothering you.'

'What should that question be?' asked the Inspector, not wishing to be drawn, in case he was going to get some unexpected information unsolicited.

'Well, it seems to me that in fiction, at least, the obvious person to look for is the last person to see the deceased alive. This must be difficult. Like doing any sort of research, I suppose. The paper you're reading will always give you references to work done before it, but obviously it is difficult to find out whether someone has done some work after the paper you have was printed. So it must be with detection. The only person who knows he *was* the last person to see the Major alive was the man who killed him. You've come back to me to ask me what you didn't ask yesterday. And the answer is that we stood outside the door of the hall waiting for the Major and the Professor to emerge. The caretaker was with us, rattling his keys and looking at his watch impatiently, as if he wanted to get away for a quick one before they closed.'

'So it was almost eleven o'clock?' put in the Inspector.

'That's right,' Duguid went on. 'When it was just eleven, (we could tell because all the clocks in the city chimed) the caretaker went inside again. A few moments later he came back and locked the doors from the inside. He lives on the

120

premises, you know. We realised that we must have missed them, so we went home. I suppose that does answer your question, doesn't it? The Major and the Professor must have slipped out by some back way together.'

'Thank you very much; that was what we wanted to know,' admitted the Inspector. Realising how helpful the male Duguid was when interviewed on his own, he decided to see what else he might discover. 'I wonder whether you have any ideas which might be of help to us. Quite honestly, we have found no reason why anyone should want to do away with the Major.'

'I have wondered about that myself,' answered Duguid. 'You only told us last night you had reason to believe that Forbes's death was not an accident, and that foul play could not be ruled out. Would you care to enlighten me a bit more?'

The Inspector, having warned the Scot that whatever he was told was confidential, then gave him as much information as he thought necessary. He did not tell Duguid why the Major had gone down the well, or how they thought the crime had been committed. Nor did he mention the state of undress of the body. A simple story that the Major was drowned in the well, that there were no signs of violence, and that the ladder had been removed and the doors propped open.

'Well, isn't that the oddest thing you ever heard?' observed Duguid. 'How on earth did they get him down there?'

'I'm afraid that we are not in a position to discuss that aspect of the case,' said the Inspector, feeling that he had probably said too much as it was.

'It certainly seems very suspicious,' said the Scot, turning round in his seat and pushing an electric plug into a wall socket. 'I'll agree that it's worth investigating. I can see why you should want to find someone who wanted the old man dead. Not that I think I'm in a position to help you much.

121

Do you mind if I ask a few questions, just to clear the ground? You can always say "no comment" if you feel I'm speaking out of turn.'

'Try me and see,' said the Inspector.

'Does anyone gain financially from the Major's death?'

'No.'

'I don't for one moment think it possible, but might he have had some hold on somebody? Blackmail is a nasty word, I know.'

'Who are you thinking of?'

'Please, don't misunderstand me. I can't imagine Forbes doing anything so nasty. He struck me as being a very honest old man. But he must have had a past, and anything is possible.'

'There is no evidence to support the theory that he was a blackmailer, or, come to that, that he was being blackmailed. As for his past, we have had our usual check made on his background. He seems to have been pretty lonely, like the old man who said that he had no enemies. When he was congratulated on this he said he'd outlived every one of the bastards. He seems to have served abroad up to his retirement, and not to have made friends afterwards. He might almost have been said not to have had a past.'

'That disposes of two of the usual motives,' said the Duguid. 'Only other one that seems to crop up in my mind is jealousy. I really can't see him being involved in a *crime passionelle* though. Twenty years ago, perhaps, or even ten, but not now.'

Steam suddenly rose behind Duguid's chair. He turned round again, opened a filing cabinet, and took out a teapot, milk bottle, sugar packet, cups and a box of biscuits. He measured tea carefully into the pot from a tobacco jar that stood on the bookcase.

'Help yourselves to sugar,' he said, when he had poured water into the pot from the electric kettle which he kept on the floor of his office. 'Now where was I? Looking for, and dismissing, motives for murdering the Major. You know, I'm stuck.' He filled their cups with tea and added the milk afterwards. 'I suppose everyone ought to be asked to comment on a crime from the point of view of their own expertise. For example, I imagine that Mr Wood's function in this matter,' he added, smiling at Peter, 'is to advise the police on the archaeological implications of the crime. I know you're not a plain clothes man. I've often seen you mud-grubbing on a dig. I've also been to a few of your lectures.'

'Touché,' said Peter, joining in the conversation. 'What is your particular line of work?'

'I suppose I'd be called an engineer, principally. What we do here is make moulds—for plastic objects. An expensive and extremely accurate business. If you look at one of those little plastic men that you can buy, you know, cowboys and indians or soldiers, you will recognise the detail with which they are made. Incredibly fine by standards of the past. Yet the toys are so cheap. The reason is, of course, that the materials are very, very cheap, and millions of any item can be made in a short time. The actual mould may take up to a thousand pounds to make.'

Peter sipped his tea. 'What would you add to our investigation, if you were asked to join us—'

'Which you won't be, so don't worry,' put in the Inspector.

'Superficially at least, I suppose my contribution ought to be an examination of detail. The only thing which is essential to us is accuracy. Everything must fit exactly to a hundredth of a millimetre here.'

'Peter here is rather averse to accuracy, you know,' said the Inspector.

'Rather a peculiar admission in an archaeologist who is also a chemistry teacher, isn't it?' asked Duguid.

'It's not accuracy that I'm against,' protested Peter. 'What I object to is what I call pseudo-accuracy, by which I mean the expression of the area of a wall to the nearest square inch, when you only need it, or even know it, to the nearest roll of wallpaper. I also object to the measurement of data simply because they are susceptible to measurement. Like, for example, reporting the weight of a corroded coin, that was very worn before it was buried, to the nearest milligramme.'

'I agree with you there,' said Duguid, 'but often we have to record every datum we can just in case it should prove useful at some future date.'

'There's not much we can measure about this particular crime, is there?' asked the Inspector. 'After all, the scene of the crime was recorded photographically by experts. We know the well was about eight feet deep, and impossible to climb into or out of—I should think that datum is quite sufficiently accurate for our purposes.'

'Perhaps it is not accuracy that is at fault,' said the engineer, gathering the cups together in a tray labelled 'out'. 'Perhaps it's detail. Or the accuracy or fit of the evidence?'

'Speaking of detail, by the way, Peter,' said the Inspector, 'I forgot to tell you. We did manage to prove that the Major was drowned in the well and not elsewhere.'

'Was there any doubt of that?'

'None at all. But it's just as well to know. The water in the lungs contained exactly the same algae and diatoms as the well did. Just an example of detail!'

'I still can't see what sort of detail we can be after here, whatever you say,' said Peter.

'That's the trouble with detection, as well as with archaeology. You never know what little detail might prove important. It might not matter that Mr Duguid is left-handed, that he chews his pen or that he broke his shoelace this morning and tied a knot in it. These are all little details—'

'Which are, I can assure you, quite irrelevant to your enquiry,' put in Duguid. 'I still say if I were a detective, I should look for some little detail that didn't fit, or some measurable quantity that didn't quite add up.'

'Perhaps you're right,' said the Inspector. 'We'll remember that.'

They rose, shook hands and were ushered out.

As they turned north along the A7 towards Broadchester, they were both silent for a time. Peter was thinking of what Duguid had said, about asking everyone involved in the case to analyse it from the point of view of their own particular specialist knowledge. It was a quaint idea, that, until you tried to apply it. Then you came unstuck, at least as a mental exercise. Dr Broad—smart doctor and specialist in heraldry and protocol. What could he have to offer? Medical evidence? They'd already got that, for what it was worth. Heraldry and protocol? Perhaps he might describe the crime in heraldric terms : 'in a well, a Major drowned, improper.'

What could Bill Denny offer? At least he should be good at making evidence dovetail; someone had used that metaphor already. He might examine the ladder as an artifact. Not much use there. He ran his mind down the list; curator, lawyer, architect, headmaster, historical novelist. . .

Funny thing, he thought, that we seem to have been talking about accuracy and detail all the morning so far. It's strange how something like that happens, almost as if there is an idea in the air, waiting to be picked up and used. It happens all the time, he thought. Words read for the first time always leap out of the next page you pick up, and objects which you see for the first time taken from the ground on a dig are either the first thing you see next time you go to a museum, or else you hear that someone else has just found one on another dig. Perhaps it was an omen, and he should think about accuracy in investigation.

'Funny that Duguid should raise the question of accuracy and detail after what we'd been talking about on the way down,' said the Inspector, suddenly. Peter found himself wondering what mental route had brought his friend's thoughts full circle.

'Ah, here's Durford,' he said, rousing himself. 'There's a lot of Roman tiles in the church tower here, and there must be some buildings here that were robbed to provide them. Someone ought to come here and do some searching about. The coaching inn over there, *the Roebuck*, ought to make a good centre, if you had the money. Nothing like fieldwork to give you an expensive appetite! Where are we going?'

'Just to check on a detail. Perhaps it's not a measurable one, but it should give us a bit more accuracy. Shire Hall; to see the caretaker.'

The Shire Hall, at Broadchester, was a Georgian building standing proudly with its columns and pediment high at the end of the market place, which now served only as a car park. Ken Harris parked the car in the square and they walked over to the hall. The imposing steps up to the colonnaded front, suggesting a temple standing on its podium, were in fact a sham. There were no doors on this side at all; the main entrance was at the back, in a cul-de-sac. The Inspector did not go round to the back, but went straight to the left hand side and led the way down steep area steps. At the bottom he knocked at a door. It was opened almost immediately by a grey-haired man in braces, shirtsleeves and no collar, who was in need of a shave. The loud sound of a radio tuned to pop music flooded into the area, so that the conversation began at a shout.

'Hello! Tom lad! Can we come in and have a word?'

'Watcher, Ken. I'll put the kettle on.'

The man went in, and they followed him into a tiny subterranean scullery, which had that strong smell of drains, soap and wet draining boards that reminded Peter of his childhood in a farm cottage. The wireless was extinguished, although Ken and Tom didn't seem to moderate their voices much.

'Don't bother about the tea, Tom; we've just been out

126

drinking with a client,' said Ken.

'What do you think I can tell you after all these years?'

'An easy one this time. I want to know what happened at the end of the archaeological meeting last Saturday evening. Did you have any difficulty turning them out, for instance?'

'All right, old cock, don't tell me anything. No trouble, but they made me miss my pint, slipping out the back way like that.'

'Who did?'

'One of them was that Major fellow; you know, the one what did that archaeological diggings over near Natford.'

'Forbes?' put in Ken.

'That's the finger. The other one was a tall bloke, fuzzy side-whiskers, flowery shirt. There was a couple waiting outside, Scottish pair, I would say. Called him "The Professor"; said they was awaiting him. I waited till closing time, and went in to give'em a bit of my mind, I can tell you.

'When I got there, they was gone. They'd pushed open one of the emergency doors—we don't leave them open except for public meetings, you know—and then slipped off down the back staircase. You know, the one that the old judge creeps up on assizes so 'e won't offend 's nostrils with the pong of all them common people.'

'I know the one—opens into Goose Lane.'

'You have it! There you are then. I just locked up, and 'ad to make do with bottled beer. What's it all about?'

'Under your hat, Tom. The old finger got himself done that night. You've done the Force proud. Buy yourself a drink.' He pushed something into the old man's hand, and they slipped out into the fresh air.

'Ex-rozzer. Crime squad—got into some rough-house down at the docks—right out of his patch altogether. Didn't say much about it afterwards. When he came round a week after, they found he was almost totally deaf. It's got a bit better and they don't seem to mind it in a good caretaker,' Ken explained.

CHAPTER 17

The Professor

Ken Harris sat in the corner of a first class railway carriage, which his rank and the ticket he carried permitted him to do, and thought slightly savage thoughts. People just didn't seem reasonable, he decided. Peter behaved like a ruddy girl friend. There had been such a rush to catch the train, and he wasn't at all sure whether they would allow his expenses to include a civilian all the way to Hinkeaton. Come to think of it, he wasn't sure whether they would even be happy about his own galavanting off on the spur of the moment like that. It would be different if he had any clear idea what it was that he intended to achieve. He had hoped that Peter might come up with some ideas, but all he'd said was, 'That's all right, I've got lots of useful work to do' and then rushed off and left him on the station. Just as well they hadn't stopped to argue, or he'd have missed one of the few trains that went across to Hinkeaton Junction. If he'd missed that one he'd have had to go down to London and back out again. There was no doubt about it though; it reminded him of the time of that last leave he'd had in the services, when he'd had to stay to pacify Mary, and finished the night sleeping in a waiting room at Trent or somewhere. The thought of his wife changed his mood rapidly, and he realised he was smiling. He looked up and caught the eye of the other inhabitant of the compartment, and tried to look as though he hadn't meant the smile for her.

At least he didn't need Peter with him to tell him which phylum of archaeologist he was going to be dealing with. This one would be clearly identified by its field markings and behaviour as academic. What slanderous summary had Peter made of the academic archaeologists? Curious birds, living in ivory towers, spending most of their time reorganising the work that other people have done; do excavate, in immaculate confusion. Chief crimes against them were plagiarism, overt confusion, or incomplete research. Not much chance of Forbes having committed one of those crimes though, from what people said of him: no motive there.

This particular specimen of the academic had already been outlined by some of the witnesses. The impression obtained was of someone very competent, but not inspired or original. A good memory, could quote large chunks of Latin, and also lists of Romano-British place names from something called an itinerary. Made a fetish of accurate, if unnecessary, recording. Sounded like a description of a detective who would never rise above sergeant, apart from the Latin.

He grinned fiercely at this thought, and looked up to catch the eye of the young lady opposite. Composing his face quickly, he opened his briefcase and began to fetch out the already voluminous file on the case. He turned to Charleston's statement and read through it. The Professor had arrived at the station in Broadchester at five forty-five or thereabouts, and was met by Mr Duguid, who took him back to have dinner at the Duguid residence. Taken on to the meeting, he had gone straight to the man who was working the projector and shown him the slides and how they were to be projected. He had then had a short word with Lady Forster whom he knew slightly from her visit to his excavation at Water End. She had introduced him to the meeting, and he had talked for over an hour. Questions afterwards, and he did remember that Forbes, whom he also knew, had asked a question about the Antonine Itinerary. He had answered it. Coffee had been served after the questions and he had talked to various people about archaeological matters. At the end of the meeting, he was discussing the paper with Major Forbes when he had realised how late it was, and he had hurried out of the hall at about eleven o'clock.

There didn't seem to be anything wrong with this statement, as far as it went. It did make the Professor the last person known to have seen the Major alive, however. No significance could be attached to the omission of the statement to say whether the Major had left with the Professor. It was a point worth raising. He could only excuse this journey on the grounds that the Professor was the most important witness they had. A pretty poor best.

The Inspector looked at the small booklet attached to the corner of the statement. It was a single postcard-sized sheet of card, folded in half, like a membership card for a small club or society. On the front it was labelled 'British Rail (North Region). Summary of services between Hinkeaton and London (St Pancras)'. Inside were the usual masses of figures in neat columns, with additional signs, symbols and abbreviations. After a long study of the booklet, and a series of false starts, Ken managed to find a train with the necessary symbols and abbreviations that told him that the train ran on Saturdays only, had a buffet car after Bletchley, and travelled via Broadchester, arriving there at 17.45 hrs. He marked this entry in red biro. It was jolly efficient of whoever took this statement to add the timetable, but damned lazy of them not to mark the trains.

A further search of the timetable produced a return train leaving Broadchester at 23.22 hrs, arriving at Hinkeaton at 02.50 hrs the following morning. No buffet on that one. Perhaps Charleston stoked up on coffee and biscuits at the meeting. There was no train after the 23.22 until nearly eight on Sunday. No wonder the Professor had seen fit to bolt out through the back door, to avoid the Duguids.

For a long while Ken looked at the Professor's statement, and thought about detail and accuracy, which had been so much in the air that morning. There didn't seem much need for accuracy. The times given were near enough, and the last

130

one tallied with what had already been established, eleven pm. The other time, that of arrival could be checked with Mr Duguid, although it was unimportant. Unimportant details were easier to think of and more entertaining: What did Mrs Duguid give them for dinner—haggis or chile con carne? What did they talk about over the meal? These details and others could be fascinating to the gossip, but of little use to the detective. Perhaps a better knowledge of what the Major had last said might be valuable, if only in revealing his state of mind.

The rest of the journey was spent quite industriously, correlating the statements made so far. As the train pulled into Hinkeaton Junction, he was pleased to see that the local constabulary had not thought it necessary to honour his visit by anything other than the assistance of a uniformed sergeant, who was standing on the platform. He was large, confident and, from his accent when they introduced themselves, a local man. On the way to the University, the sergeant told the Inspector that it was he who had been responsible for the statement taken from the Professor, and the attached timetable.

'I think that a uniformed sergeant is quite enough for them up at the University,' said the sergeant, without rancour. 'We don't want them thinking they're too important, if you get me, or there'll be no holding them.'

The great advantage of having the sergeant drive him to the University, Ken thought, was that he didn't have to decide which one of the many isolated architectural monstrosities he would have to go to. The car drove straight to the front door of one of them, while Ken mused over what Peter would say about all this rectilinear architecture.

'The Professor is expecting us, sir,' said the sergeant. 'I took the liberty of making an appointment, since you did say over the phone that this was a courtesy call and nothing more. I hope I did right?'

'Yes thanks, sergeant; I didn't want to surprise him, or to

131

find that he was out.'

They entered a lift that was a little bigger than a fitted wardrobe, which at the touch of a button sped them up to the top floor of the building, which a sign pronounced to be the situation of the Senior Common Room. Sixteen floors above the ground, they emerged from the lift into a vestibule. Through double glass doors they could see into a large room, equipped with large padded chairs, magazine racks and writing tables rather like the members' room in a London club, as far as the furnishings went. The main differences were the modernity of the design of the chairs and the bright orange carpet on the floor, and above all, the astonishing absence of far wall. From where the policemen stood, the room apparently ended in the clouds. The Inspector stood, wondering what they should do now.

'You did get the place right, I suppose?' he asked the sergeant.

'That's right, sir. He said he'd meet us at the Senior Common Room and we were to come straight up.'

The doors opened and through them came a tall, thin, rather boyish looking man. He had bushy side whiskers and a shirt that even Peter Wood might have envied, with matching tie. Apart from these extravagances, the newcomer, who greeted the sergeant as an old friend, appeared quite conventional. Dark suit, black shoes, short haircut. Ken decided he was nearer to forty than thirty.

'How do you do, Inspector,' said the Professor when they were formally introduced. 'Come on in. There's hardly anyone about yet, as we don't come up for a couple of weeks yet.'

As they went into the lounge, or whatever it should be called, Ken realised that the expression to 'come up' had a special university meaning here, not at all connected with the lift to the sixteenth floor.

'The coffee bar is always open,' the Professor went on, leading them through a self-service bar, and paying for their coffee and buns on the way out. 'That's why I thought you'd like to come up. The view is worth seeing anyway.'

He led them to a table against what should have been the far wall. Ken found himself sitting against a plate glass window which sloped outwards into space from the floor, so that he could look straight down into the car park nearly two hundred feet below. On the far side of the car park was a municipal cemetery. It was amusing to see that from this height, the parked cars and the graves parodied one another. He tried to concentrate on the Professor.

'I'm sorry to bother you like this, Professor. From the statements we have taken so far, it appears that you are the last person to have admitted to seeing Major Forbes, the archaeologist, alive and well. That fact alone makes you of some importance in the enquiry, even though he died some time after you left him.'

'What time did he actually die, Inspector, and how?'

'For various reasons I cannot give you all the details, Professor, but it is common knowledge that he was drowned, in the well at Cold Beech Villa at about midnight, or a little after, on the night of the meeting you addressed.'

'I see.' The Professor twirled one of his side whiskers thoughtfully. 'At least that lets me out. I was away just after eleven.'

'You caught the eleven twenty-two from Broadchester.'

'That's right. I was talking to the Major—we have met before, and even corresponded at one time—when I realised how time was pressing. I knew that Mr and Mrs Duguid would be waiting for me. Charming people, but a bit like treacle, sweet and adhesive. I went so far as to point this out to the Major. He was most understanding. Even said that he would act as a decoy if necessary. Then he remembered that there was an emergency exit to the hall. I think it is a bolt hole for Her Majesty's Lords Justices of Assize. We nipped down there together, the Major pointed the way to the station, and I nipped off pretty sharply. He turned back to

133

get his car.'

'What were you talking to the Major about?'

'General archaeological matters, you know. Training of fieldworkers, the usefulness of archaeological qualifications and things like that. We experts can go on about these things for hours and hours.'

'Did you have anything to say about the Antonine Itinerary, at all?'

'He did mention the matter. We'd already talked it out at question time, so there wasn't much to be said.'

'Someone said to me this morning that we might find it useful in a rather diffuse enquiry like this one seems to be, to ask the witnesses what they think of the crime, if crime it was, from the point of view of their own discipline. What would you say about the Major and his death?'

'You haven't really told me what you think was the reason for the Major's death,' objected the Professor. 'Am I supposed to be explaining why he was there, why he killed himself, or who killed him?'

'Unlikely as it may sound to you,' said the Inspector, 'there seems to be a logical explanation for the Major to be where he was when he was. I'd rather not go into that just now, though. The unsolved part is how he came to be dead. There seems to be some doubt as to whether his death could have been an accident,' he added, non-commitally.

'So really, what you are asking is my opinion, as an archaeologist, for what that's worth, of the chances of the Major being done away with, or doing away with himself.' The Professor twisted his whiskers again.

'And as the person who last spoke to him, as far as we know.'

'In archaeology, we spend a lot of our time classifying, and discovering the relationship between what might be called facts, both in space and time. I don't know the details of the events which caused the death of the Major, but your presence here, my dear Inspector, suggests to me that it

134

might be thought of as a possible homicide. That's one classification dealt with. The victim, I am sure you already know, was a retired military man, very upright, with quite a reputation as a competent archaeologist. I don't know much else about him, although we had met. The murderer, if there was one, might better be described in terms of his *modus operandi*, which you have not revealed. He must have been flitting around the Ancient Monument at an unearthly hour, from what you tell me. I know the place and it is entirely enclosed. Was anything taken or disturbed?'

'No.'

'Then there is little to be said of your supposed killer, except that he must have been nocturnal. As regards the relationship of facts in space and time, I would recommend that you should examine closely your records of the position of the body and other objects; everything must be accurately recorded, I am always telling my students. Everything that can be measured must be measured. The site record is the most important document we have, and it cannot contain too many data. I hope the police are as thorough with the accuracy of their records and procedures as the archaeologists from Hinkeaton.'

'So do I,' put in the Inspector, to stem the flow and check the gallop of Charleston's hobbyhorse. 'What about the relationship of facts in time?'

'What we have to know, simply, is who could possibly have been at Cold Beech Villa in the middle of the night. Or is the time even more accurately known?'

'We can be pretty sure that it was just after twelve,' said the Inspector.

'Then all you have to do is to find out who could have been there at that time. It lets me out; I was on my way home. I took a party of foreign students on a tour of local sites next morning, so I had to be back before breakfast. It's not all sitting about at university, you know.'

'I think you over simplify our problems, you know. There

135

may be thousands of people who might have been at Cold Beech at midnight on Saturday. We have to find someone who had both the opportunity and the motive. A rare, and apparently non existent, combination,' pointed out the Inspector, rising and trying not to look at the vertiginous drop on his left. 'If you think of anything the Major may have said, please get in touch with us.'

'I'm sorry that your long journey has been wasted, Inspector,' smiled the Professor, shaking hands.

'Not at all. You've been most helpful,' said the Inspector, with more conviction in his voice than in his heart.

CHAPTER 18

Inquest

On the Thursday following Major Forbes' death, the detective and the archaeologist held what the latter called a 'council of despair' over a lunch of fish and chips in Peter's bijou residence. The detective reported what he had learned from the Professor which, he admitted, was not worth the journey.

'It's always a good idea for the man on the job to meet everyone who might have anything to offer. They didn't let me interrogate the clergy involved, but they wouldn't have much to offer if I did. They seemed to keep much to themselves and, according to their independent testimony, they were all together, discussing church business until well after midnight.'

'It looks as though the whole investigation is a blank. Nobody saw the Major, or can in any way be connected with him after the BAAAS meeting broke up at eleven,' Peter pointed out. 'Nobody seemed to have any social contact with him for weeks before the meeting. If we do have to believe that anyone had a motive for murdering him, it must have been either one of the people he spoke to at the meeting, or else it was just a passing maniac.'

'I can't see anything in any of the statements we have taken to suggest that anybody threatened, or was threatened by, the Major that evening. No-one suggested that he appeared anything other than slightly excited, as though he had just discoverd something,' said the Inspector.

'If he discovered something,' Peter observed, 'he must have discovered it at the meeting. In which case, it should have been apparent to all the people present, unless it was something either personal to the Major, or too clever for the others. In other words, he might have seen or heard something in the Professor's lecture that excited him. Like seeing an old flame in one of the slides, or recognising some archaeological object or fact which the Professor brought with him.'

'If you are right about that, it is unlikely that we shall ever know about it. Charleston didn't mention anything that the Major said that might help, neither did anyone else. If he did see something of personal interest, and didn't tell anyone, then it would be unlikely to account for his death. If he did tell someone, then they would come under suspicion, and would not be likely to tell us.' The Inspector paused. 'Come to think of it, he could have made a telephone call to anybody he cared to after the meeting. They could have come over, done the deed, and gone on their way. I don't think we would be able to discover who or why, even if we went through the Professor's lecture with a fine tooth comb—which I am not prepared to do.'

'Did anything unexpected happen in the Cold Beech–Natford area that night?'

'I've been through all the reports that I can find,' admitted the Inspector. 'As you remarked once before, the difficulty is that the man on the beat is mobile. Those bikes are quiet, but they would cover the sounds of anything other than a shot, and anyway they give the villain warning of their approach. The local man did go through Natford that night at midnight. He saw nothing moving, and the usual cars parked behind the *Fisherman's Rest*. The locals tend to use the car park there if they haven't the space themselves. The landlord doesn't seem to mind. Our man shone his torch over the cars to make sure there were not loiterers trying to break in. I wish he'd made a note of what vehicles were there. He then went on down the road, but didn't call at Cold Beech, worse luck. He says that there was a couple in a car about half a mile down the road, but they were parked off the highway and appeared to be quite busy, so he left

138

them alone. Again, he failed to make a note of the number of the car. He has been given a rocket. They might not have been occupied with sex, but with poaching. They might have been useful witnesses too. We'll never trace them now.'

'So our suspects, other than the unknown and unknowable, are those people who saw Forbes on Saturday. The BAAAS lot, in fact,' said Peter.

'If you feel like it you could include Mrs Weston in that list as well. She couldn't have done the deed, though; she's not physically strong enough to take the ladder away.'

'Let's ignore motive for a moment, and look at opportunity. Of the BAAAS lot, who could have been at Cold Beech at midnight?' Peter asked.

'Here's my little list. I don't waste train journeys.' The Inspector took a sheet of paper from his files.

'In the order in which we saw them, from statements made to the uniformed branch for us: Dr Broad, at home, in bed. Wife confirms; maid saw him come in. Bill Denny at home. Wife confirms. Ivor Jones at home. Wife confirms. Mr Hanbury at home. Wife enjoys it.'

They both giggled at the recollection. The Inspector continued.

'Miss Spratt. No alibi. Lives alone and probably dreams sinful dreams. Probably not physically or mentally adapted to this sort of crime, I should say.'

'I agree,' said Peter.

'Mr Bugg, also at home. Wife confirms. Doolittle-Smythe, the lawyer. Alone, in bed; no connection with Forbes apparent. Mr Petchy, the queer architect, lives with a "friend" who says he was home, for what that's worth. No obvious connection with Forbes. Lady Forster, at home with lots of witnesses—'

'A cloud of witness, you mean,' said Peter.

'—and two self-alibied Duguids. Add to them three mutually alibied clergy and a Lord Lieutenant who must be above suspicion, and that's the lot.'

'Except for the Prof. But he must have been on his way home by then.'

'Confirmed,' said the Inspector, 'by the fact that he was able to set out with a party of students at nine the next morning. He can't have gone off with Forbes and then rushed back to the station to catch the next train; there wasn't one till breakfast time next day, and it's a long journey. Anyway what would his motive be?'

'I don't know. I just distrust these academics. The only person who isn't covered is Doolittle-Smythe, unless we allow conspiracy,' said Peter.

'Unless some motive turns up, we are bound to admit that we have not got a case against anybody, or even enough evidence to take to a jury to say it was homicide. We're back where we were on Tuesday night. An open verdict, based on the odd circumstances of the time and place of the death, relying on the discretion of the Coroner, who is a good chap in a case like this, to cover up the even odder facts about the Major's attire. That's the best we can hope for.'

The Inspector rose and repacked his briefcase. 'I'll get on to the Coroner's officer and try to get that one through. Thanks very much for your help, Peter. I'll let you know if anything else turns up.'

The inquest was held a couple of days later, in that rather furtive way the coroners' affairs are sometimes done, which seems to negate the old principle that justice should be seen to be done. The Coroner set up his court in a back room at the Council Offices, and a small jury of seven disinterested passers-by was convened by officers who went out into the street. Evidence was called of identification. Death was found to be by drowning. Enough was said of the circumstances of the death to persuade a jury that an open verdict was in order. Altogether a quiet business.

Peter, who heard all about the inquest later from Ken Harris, was not at all surprised that whereas the obituary of the Major was given considerable prominence in the local

140

weekly paper, the report of the inquest was hidden away among the reports of jumble sales and other similar world-shattering events in the local villages.

The police enquiries, considerably toned down from the incipient murder hunt after the discovery of the fire extinguisher, continued for a couple of weeks, with the manpower involved gradually weakening in numbers. No new evidence was discovered. All the statements were cross checked, without significant result. No witness was forthcoming of the Major's last appointment at the Villa.

Peter, meanwhile, had found himself with an extensive Roman cemetery being eaten away by bulldozers, and was organising, with help from friends and pupils, a rescue operation, occupying all the hours of daylight in digging and the rest of his waking hours in cleaning and recording. Then came the beginning of his new term back at school. The problem of who killed the Major was shelved away at the back of his mind until the Christmas vacation.

CHAPTER 19

Roman Britain—sites explored

On the third day of his Christmas holiday, as Peter was busy typing a report on the Roman cemetery for the Department of the Environment, using two fingers, the postman knocked on the door. By the time Peter opened it, the postman had gone leaving behind a large flat parcel. The label bore Peter's address and the address of the sender: The Society for the Promotion of Roman Studies.

Peter retired to his study and found the paper knife, which he knew to be an essential requirement in reading the Journal of Roman Studies, not merely to obtain access to the interior of the tightly wrapped parcel, but also to get into the letterpress. The JRS was a prestige publication, and one of the ways in which this manifested itself was in the fact that the pages were left uncut. It was, of course, assumed that subscribers would have the volume bound uniformly with the rest of their library and trimmed by their bookbinders, before they attempted to read the contents.

Peter carefully slit the journal open at the few pages which, in his opinion, made the whole thing worth buying. Ignoring the discussions on 'Roman Jurisprudence in the Provinces' and the 'Use of Greek Epithets among Minor Roman Playwrights', he opened the work at 'Sites explored'. Here was to be found a very brief abstract of all the excavations which had occurred in Britain for the year before on Roman sites. Often, with the more important sites, a plan was included. He turned to the work done on Broadshire, and was pleased to find his own excavations accurately recorded, along with others by the museums and by the Major. Also included was a short note on the work which Professor Charleston had done at Water End and a whole-

142

page plan, rather too much reduced, of the area of excavation.

Taking out a magnifying glass, he examined the plan carefully. On his last evening on earth, Major Forbes had seen a slide prepared from this plan, on a screen at a meeting of the BAAAS. Either something he had seen, or something he had heard said at the meeting had caused the Major to behave as though—what was it Denny had said? As though some great truth had been revealed to him alone? What had he seen that others had missed? The site appeared to have consisted mostly of timber buildings, whose presence was evidenced by rectangular arrangements of postholes in the subsoil, and areas of cobbled paths between them. In one corner of the excavated area, in a rather frustrating way, there were traces of a proper masonry structure shown. Peter wondered what sort of building it could be, and why it had not been fully excavated at the time. Perhaps it was a find late in the season, going under the Prof's spoil heaps.

He felt sure that there was something in this excavation which would tell him about the Major's state of mind shortly before he died. It might not tell why he died, or who was responsible, if anyone was, but it would reveal something that might otherwise be lost. If Forbes did discover something about the site, he really ought to know what it was.

The idea did not occur to Peter while he was looking at the note or plan. It came later when he read the second part of the notes on Roman Britain—'Inscriptions'. Under Broadshire, there was only a couple of notes. The first was a note of the name 'JVLI' scratched on a samian bowl from one of the sites dug by a museum. The other was a report of several letters, cut from sheet bronze, found at Water End. They were four inches high, showed no sign of any fastening, and were found in an undoubted Roman context. They could be regarded as an anagram, with no prospect of

143

solution.

The discovery of the letters, or rather of the existence of the letters, was of considerable interest to Peter. He remembered the time when he had made a similar discovery at a riverside site during work in advance of the construction of a new trunk road. He turned up the reference in his filing system. There it was: similar letters had been found at Dicket Mead, Springhead, Woodeaton, Cirencester, Lydney. They had been described as 'votive letters', since the one thing that the findspots had in common was that they were temple sites.

He turned back the page to the plan of the Water End excavation. That masonry structure which disappeared under the side of the Prof's trench. What shape could it have been? Two walls, running parallel about fifteen feet apart across the corner of the trench. The outer one, that is the one of which the greater length was exposed, appeared to turn at right angles just before it reached the end of the excavation. He made a quick sketch on a piece of tracing paper and then superimposed it onto the plan. It was possible at least, he discovered, that the walls were part of the ambulatory of a temple. He had seen often enough the plans of the so-called 'Romano-Celtic temples', which appeared to consist of two concentric squares, the inner one, the *cella*, being the actual room containing the holy of holies, surrounded by an ambulatory, a covered walk-way—like cloisters turned inside out.

Perhaps that was what the Major had seen that the Professor had missed. Why, then, had neither of them actually said anything about it? The witnesses were fairly clear in their evidence. The question the Major had asked was about the Antonine Itinerary—*Iter* XVII, if Taffy the Museum was correct. Could Water End have been a stage on the road? The Professor had demolished the idea by quoting the *Iter* involved, and pointing out that the route was already known to lie under the present A7 trunk road.

Peter fetched out the map of the area from a drawer. The route of the A7 did a distinct kink to the east of Water End, passing over a mile away. With a ruler laid on the map, he found that the line of the Roman road from the south could be extrapolated through Water End, and only a short diversion would bring it back onto the alignment to the north. The obvious reason for the diversion of the present trunk road was that it forded the small river at Durford. Was it possible that the A7 was on the line of a later road than the Roman one, or that the Roman road itself originally went through Durford but was diverted through Water End by the time of the Itinerary?

An hour later, Peter's desk was covered with his usual purposeful chaos. The map and journal had been joined by air photographs, tithe maps, gazeteers and site reports. His previous work was forgotten. So was the murder enquiry. He was filled with that restless excitement which marks the true fieldworker. He picked up the telephone and dialled a Broadchester number. He was rewarded by the squeaky voice of Bill Denny. He identified himself.

'What's up then, old son? Another crash-bang-wallop-who's-got-the-pot dig for us?'

'As a matter of fact,' said Peter, 'I want to go out and trace a Roman road. Care to come along?'

'I don't believe in Roman roads, you know that. Chasing imaginary straight lines about all over the countryside is a good, healthy pastime for aged eccentrics, and quite harmless,' said Bill. 'And what's more, I don't think anyone learnt anything from a Roman road except that it might be there. You can infer the existence of a road from the settlement pattern, but no-one ever deduced the settlement pattern from the roads.'

'This one's different,' said Peter with conviction. 'It is part of an itinerary we're trying to unravel. Anyway, if you leave that ruddy cabinet-making and come straight over, we'll be in time for lunch at *the Roebuck* in Durford.'

'Lovely grub! I suppose you're treating me?'

'Of course. See you in half an hour.'

On the way to Durford, Peter explained his idea about the Itinerary and the possibility of Water End being on the alignment of the Roman road.

'But what's all this got to do with the excavation that old Charleston did, and what was Forbes blithering about when he asked his question at that meeting? He didn't ask anything about a possible temple site, only about the *iter*.'

'That's the real payoff,' said Peter. 'I think it was a rather esoteric game that Forbes and Charleston played in front of the audience. I wouldn't mind betting that Forbes knew the seventeenth *iter* as well as Charleston did. Instead of standing up and scoring off the Prof by asking outright if he'd noticed the significance of the arrangement of the walls in the trench, and the bronze letters which he'd hung up, he asked an oblique question which would go over the heads of most, if not all, of the audience. I think what he asked was something like: "Could the site at Water End have constituted the end of the tenth stage of the seventeenth *iter* of the Antonine Itinerary?" The Professor would be one of the very few people who could run through the *iter* in his head, naming the stops—'

'Like asking someone who is fairly hot stuff on theology if he thought that the third commandment was as important now as it was in its contemporary society?' Bill butted in.

'More esoteric and subtle than that. Do you know the name of the Roman town which should appear about where Durford is?'

'Come off it, old son,' pleaded Bill. 'I'm a ruddy dirt archaeologist, not one of your fat-gutted desk excavators. I know where to find the information if I wanted to. Which I wouldn't. I'm not likely to dig up anyone who can tell me the way, even if I did know the name of the ruddy place.'

'It was Pognemton,' said Peter.

'Lovely Celtic word!' chortled Bill. 'What's it mean then?

146

Surely not the home of the bog dwellers?'

'I don't know about the first half of the word,' admitted Peter, 'but the second half would have meant something to a professor, if not a dirt archaeologist. There are several examples of places called something-*nemeton* in Roman Britain. "Nemeton" is the Celtic name for one of their sacred groves. So Pognemeton could easily be a slovenly contracted form of the sacred grove of Pog, or Bog if you like. I bet he saw the connection almost immediately, and had a quick debate whether to agree with Forbes or not. Then he realised that he couldn't very well agree outright. I expect his report was already with the editor of whatever journal is going to publish it, and anyway he had already told lots of people about the site without himself twigging onto the significance of the temple walls. So he would probably cover up, and then have a chat with Forbes afterwards. He might even have suggested to him that he had seen the significance but had kept it a secret to avoid treasure seekers spudding about. Something along those lines.'

'Perhaps he decided that he'd have to do old Freddie in to stop his blathering!' suggested Bill, jokingly.

'What a lovely idea!' agreed Peter. 'Still, it's not a very good motive. I can't imagine Alan Charleston confessing "I done it, Inspector, to prevent him from saying he'd found my Roman temple!" He'd never know when someone else would come up with the same idea. I just don't believe it. All he'd have to do is say, "Hush, don't breathe a word to a soul—I'm planning a big dig at it next year", and all would be bright and smiling. I'll pop up and have a chat with the Prof myself this week. Perhaps he'll try to do me in. Then you can go and tell all to Ken Harris, so that I will not have died in vain.'

As he spoke they pulled into the car park of the *Roebuck Inn*, on the coaching road through Durford, and they forgot archaeology for the more immediate prospect of a four-star lunch.

CHAPTER 20

Fieldwork

There is really no occupation so thoroughly absorbing physically and mentally as archaeological fieldwork. It is always rewarding, even when the rewards are mere serendipity, the accidental discoveries which occur when a piece of landscape is intensively studied.

Bill Denny and Peter Wood spent the short afternoon with map and boots, walking along the suggested alignment of the Roman road through Water End. Both Peter and Bill were very cynical about Roman roads. They both knew that it was possible to produce what might be called evidence of the existence of a road on any arbitrary line on the map. Peter had even tried the experiment with his digging group one winter's day. Without telling them, he had thrown a long ruler down on a two-and-a-half inch map, and then drawn a line beside it. He had then given the map to the group and sent them off to trace the alignment of a road. They had reported that the alignment marked was slightly to the south of the true one, and that there were several minor realignments. There was distinct evidence, however, of aggers, metalling and all the usual touchstones of Roman main roads. No-one had asked where the road was going from and to, and the group were resentful at being hoaxed.

Among the serendipity which came their way that afternoon was a fine collection of worked flints from a ploughed field, ('I don't expect the Roman road adherents would believe in these,' Bill pointed out,) a previously unmarked moated site, a quick flash of a kingfisher down by the river, and a bunch of fullers' teazles which, despite their early importance in carding and napping in the woollen industries, are now comparatively rare. Peter collected some seeds to plant in his garden.

By the time they had reached Water End, they were both ready to admit that the possibility of a road through the line they had walked was a very good one. Even the most cynical would have to admit that the existence of the road had been possibly established, and definitely not disproved. They passed the site of Professor Charleston's excavations, inefficiently backfilled, and now covered in the remains of thistles and ragwort.

'Let's go and see if we can pick up a few coins from his spoil heaps,' suggested Bill, maliciously.

'Definitely not sporting. Anyway, we've got work to do yet,' rejoined Peter. 'There is one thing which will make or mar our theory. If there was a road through, there must have been a ford. Let's go and see.'

One very eminent field historian has suggested that archaeologists should be divided into two categories, the farmerphobes and the farmerphiles. The farmerphobes are the ones who try to make whatever investigation they are engaged upon without contact with the locals, preferring to make their own decisions, without suggestions from people who are unable to distinguish between Queen Elizabeth and Queen Victoria, and who are unable to believe that the Romans didn't come just before their grandfathers started steam ploughing. The farmerphiles, on the other hand, prefer to go straight to the farm, risking the waste of time spent in sifting the garbled history and legend so obtained, and gaining the benefit that, if the natives are friendly, they will be able to walk more or less freely without being set upon for trespassing.

Peter's experience had led him into a middle path. It is often difficult to discover who owns a field. If you stand in it, however, it is rare for anyone to challenge you—and if they do, you have found the owner. Also, it is better to have a surreptitious look at a site before asking permission. If permission is refused, you have at least had a perfunctory inspection. If it is granted, then you can make a proper survey. On that cold December afternoon, Peter found that he had been cast by fate in the role of -phile rather than -phobe. The farm, Perryman's Farm, was close to the river and any surreptitious search for a ford was not possible.

'Pity, it'll be getting dark very shortly. Let's try to get away without too much gossip,' suggested Peter.

They knocked on the farmhouse door. After a short wait, it was opened by a man as large as Bill Denny. Ginger hair and moustache, bright blue eyes. Stockinged feet on the brick floor. Peter saw the rubber boots in the corner beside the door.

'What can I do for you gentlemen?' asked the farmer, very politely.

Peter explained that they were following the line of a supposed Roman road, and asked permission to walk along the river to look for a ford. He was somewhat surprised by the direct nature of the reply.

'Of course. The old Roman ford is just over there, behind that willow tree. My father and the old rector were quite sure it was on the line. There's a proper causeway leading to it. That's why three-acre there is never ploughed—there's a great band of stone right across the middle of it. But you won't want to hang about; the light's going. Pop over and have a look and then come back and have a cup of tea; we're just brewing up now.'

There could be no doubt that there was a possible ford at Perryman's Farm. Just where the farmer had indicated, the river widened and then became shallow. The soft banks were replaced by a layer of compacted flints. Peter and Bill walked over the river and back, without even having to slow down to prevent the water coming over the tops of their wellingtons. Still standing in the river, they shook hands solemnly.

'Under the bloody A7 my foot,' said Bill impolitely, 'and now I could do with that cup of farmhouse tea. I suppose

150

we'll have to pay for it by being bored to death.'

Back in the farmhouse they were ushered, on stockinged feet, into an enormous living-room-kitchen, whose fireplace belied the apparent Victorian exterior of the farm. They were introduced to the farmer's wife, who was quite unlike anything they might have expected, being small and angular and rather birdlike in her movements. They accepted cake spread with strawberry jam and large mugs of thick brown tea, and sat in what appeared to be a church pew standing opposite the fireplace.

'That's a fine fire there,' said Peter, 'and a lovely ingle fireplace. Rather surprising in this building, isn't it?'

'Ah! There's a story about that,' said the farmer. 'The original farm was burnt down about 1830 or thereabouts. As far as I can gather, the farmer himself was killed in the fire. His daughter had married the son of a neighbouring farmer, and for a while this farm was worked from the neighbouring farm, while they saved up to rebuild. The chimney of the old place remained standing for about twenty years; then, with inherited and saved money, they built the present place around the old ingle fireplace. That's how it comes to be Perryman's. That was her married name. She was my great-great-grandmother. Just a moment.' He left the room and Bill and Peter toasted themselves in front of the roaring fire.

'Here you are. This is the farm that was burned down.' He handed a small framed print to Bill. Peter looked over his shoulder.

'What a pity it went,' Bill observed. 'Lovely bit of timber framing there. Quite clearly mediaeval. You can see that the bedroom windows are insertions into a single-storied hall. It's a pity it went,' he repeated.

Peter made the right sort of appreciative noises. Timber-framed buildings were something which he had a feeling for, but very little knowledge of. He thought the picture itself was quite interesting too. He examined it closely and realised that it was not a print but the original drawing, which must have survived the fire because it was a treasured memento belonging to the farmer's married daughter over 130 years before. How had it come into existence? He looked closely for the signature at the bottom. What a pity. Artist unknown. He turned the picture over and looked at the back. Written on the brown paper which covered it, in spidery black copper-plate writing, were the words 'Bogington Hall Farm 1792'.

'Well I'm damned!' he said aloud.

'What's the matter?' asked the farmer and Bill, together.

'Look at the name of the building in this picture. See— here on the back of it. "Bogington Hall". The building disappeared too early to appear on any of the old maps of the area, and then reappeared with a new name. Even if the place name people had got hold of it, I suppose they would have invented some Saxon called Bog. An -ingas place name, or the town of the folk of Bog. We start our research from a different end. We were looking for Pognemton. See it? Pognemeton, Pognemton, Bogington. Just imagine the name remaining unchanged all that time.'

He carefully explained the significance of the discovery to the farmer.

'I can't see what all the fuss is about. I remember my old dad being told that by the rector when I was a lad. He always said that there should have been an old temple just the other side of what we've always called Roman's Ford—the ford that you just went and looked at before tea. I thought that was why those stuck-up people from Hinkeaton University came down here to dig in Tile Mead. Mind you, they never discussed it with me and apart from writing to ask for a short lease on the field, which ends this year incidentally, they've left me alone. As far as I know, I've never had a chance to speak to one of them. They believe in keeping to themselves.'

'You know, I think the farmerphobes miss quite a lot,' said Peter, with feeling. He accepted another cup of tea from this intelligent farmer, and explained *that* remark.

CHAPTER 21

The Department of Roman Studies

The following day, Peter drove up the motorway to Hinkeaton. He hoped that the Professor of Roman Studies would be in the city, if not actually in the University. He drove straight to the University which he knew had begun as a large mansion in its own grounds, grounds which were now alas filled with tall concrete and glass tower blocks. The mansion offered the best chance, he thought, bewildered by the signposts. They merely indicated the way to the blocks, using the names of the various benefactors, he supposed, rather than their functions or the faculties they served. What went on, he wondered, in the Frederick Stacey Block, or the Natchbull-Twee Building?

Inside the main entrance of the original Queen Anne mansion was a desk manned by two uniformed guards.

'I've come to see Professor Charleston—the archaeologist,' he explained.

'Do you have an appointment, sir?' asked one of the guards.

'No, I was just passing through and wondered if he might be in today,' fibbed Peter.

The man picked up a phone and dialled. After a wait, he spoke.

'Is himself in?' he asked. 'Visitor. A Mr -?'

'Wood. Peter Wood.'

'A Mr Peter Wood. Says he was just passing. O.K.' He put the phone down. 'Just wait a moment. They're coming to fetch you.'

Swing doors at the side of the entrance hall opened and through them came a young lady. As she walked up to him, Peter looked at her with frank admiration. She was about twenty-five, he guessed, and her well-proportioned construction was emphasised, rather than concealed, by the roll-necked pullover and tight jeans that she was wearing. Her face could not be said to be beautiful, so much as pretty. Intelligent blue eyes, he supposed, would always be pretty. Perhaps her lower lip was a bit too full. Her mouth and face were totally devoid of make up. It wasn't needed, he thought. Her face was heart-shaped and framed by a mass of long blonde hair.

'Ah! Mr Wood!' she said, as if she had known him all her life, and extended a hand for him to shake. 'I'm Sheila Snell, the Professor's research assistant. Would you care to follow me down into the Department?'

Peter pulled himself together sufficiently to remark that nothing would give him greater pleasure than to follow her anywhere, but specially down to the Department. And down it proved to be. In the original layout of the mansion, Peter decided, the swing doors would have marked the entrance into the domain of the butler. The Department of Roman Studies was evidently subterranian, in the ample cellars. They walked down a vaulted corridor, lighted by bulkhead lights. Miss Snell walked a few paces in front of Peter, who enjoyed the experience very much. Realising Peter was a new boy to the University, she remarked, referring to the architecture and not to what Peter was thinking about, 'Cool in summer, warm in winter, and damp at all times.'

Miss Snell's room was partitioned from a large cellar which was full of metal shelves stacked with shoeboxes to hold pottery from digs. There were still racks on the walls of the office, once intended to hold bottles, now holding stacks of rolled papers, maps, plans and drawings.

'How can we help you?' asked Miss Snell, clearing papers off a chair for Peter. 'I'm afraid that Himself hasn't come in yet. It *is* the vacation,' she explained.

'I've just come up from Broadshire,' said Peter, 'and since I am engaged in some fieldwork down there, and remembered that the Professor was himself working in the County last year, I had an idea that the Professor might be able to help. In particular, I am interested in trying to complete some of the work that the late Major Forbes was doing when he died.'

'I might be able to help you. I was doing the finds for Himself at the Water End dig. Mind you, I didn't have much to do with the report he sent to the Antiquaries this time. I usually do most of the donkey work for him, drawings, organising specialist reports and all that. Everything, in fact, but the actual text. This time he did rather hug the plans and so on to himself. Let me do the finds and see to the specialists. This time the sections and plans are in his own fair hand. You'll be able to satisfy yourself about the actual work before Christmas. The Antiquaries Journal is just being distributed. Here's the first copy.' She held up the familiar grey-covered journal. 'Do you automatically get a copy?' she asked.

'No, I have to dash up to the Antiquaries' library if I want to see one. Or buy an offprint,' he admitted.

'I'll have one sent to you when we get ours.'

'Thanks very much indeed,' said Peter, sincerely.

'Is there anything else you'd like to know? I remember he did a paper on Broadshire for the County Society last summer so we have lots of notes somewhere.' She indicated a large filing cabinet in the corner of the room.

'Can you produce anything on the Antonine Itinerary for the County?' Peter asked.

Miss Snell opened the top drawer of the filing cabinet and took out a bundle of bank foolscap, typed in double spacing and held together by a large bulldog clip. She turned to the back page which appeared to be an index, then to one of the inside pages.

'Nothing that would be news to you. The last reference given in the text of his paper was nearly twenty years old. The *iters* which go through the County are, of course, well known and no further work was needed on them.'

Peter thought to himself that this was a case of blindness caused by academic arrogance.

'You didn't go down to Broadshire when the Professor went to give his paper?' he asked.

'Not me. It took me long enough to write the damn thing and get some slides together. He'd lost his Water End slides, you know, and we had to cadge off people who had visited the site. I don't expect anyone noticed at the meeting, but the pictures were all under-prepared and few of them had proper scales. No, he gave me a lift down as far as Bedford, where I went for the weekend with my mother; he went on from there, and I made my way back on the Monday morning.'

So that was why she hadn't been there. It seemed odd that the Professor hadn't told her afterwards something about the question the Major had raised.

'Are you going back to do another season at Water End?' he asked.

'No. What we were looking for was a suitable site for a long-term investigation, preferably a villa or the like, with deep stratification and a longer period of occupation. Himself wants to spend his later years on a really long look at the whole of a site. This one just doesn't fit the bill, and he's lost interest in it.' She took up the papers and put them back in the cabinet.

'Did you ever meet the farmer at Perryman's Farm? Mr Perryman, in fact, the fourth generation. He owned the Water End site.'

The girl shook her head. 'All our contact with these people is through our legal department. We try to avoid meeting them. The dig is run as a business affair. We rent the field from them; on a two year lease in this instance. When we arrive on the site we are practically self-supporting, bringing everything we need, including provisions, with us. It's good practice for other expeditions

156

and saves a lot of time. We don't encourage hobnobbing with the peasants at all.'

Peter smiled. 'You'd be surprised what you miss that way,' he suggested. 'I've decided that farmerphobes miss a lot. You're not even farmerphobes, you're farmerfuges.'

The girl looked puzzled. 'I'm afraid I don't quite understand,' she said.

Peter was saved from explanation by the strident ringing of the telephone. The girl answered it.

'Roman Studies. Yes, hello Alan. Well, we do have a visitor. Peter Wood.' She covered the mouthpiece with her hand and spoke to Peter. 'It's the Prof. He says did you dig Pigstye Patch?' she asked. Peter nodded. Miss Snell listened for a while.

'He says if you did, he'd love to meet you, but he can't get into the University today. Can you drop in to see him this evening at about eight?' He nodded again. 'That's fine! Yes, I'll be there too. See you!'

She rang off.

'It appears that he's having a small party at his place out on Trent Road this evening, if you can make it. Nothing formal, just a few people from the University,' she explained.

'I'll see you there?' asked Peter.

'Looking forward to it. Must get on now. Can you see yourself out?'

Peter spent the rest of the morning at the museum, and the afternoon in the town, doing his Christmas shopping. It was a good shopping centre. He had a leisurely dinner in the *Bell Hotel*, and sat in the lounge to digest and waste time till the Professor's party. As he sat there, he wondered what he was trying to do. Was he investigating something, and if so, what was it? An archaeological problem, an academic mystery, or a homicide? He was sure that the evidence he and Bill had found the day before was sufficient to establish the identity of Pognemton and Water End. Perhaps sheer academic arrogance and self isolation could have concealed

157

the fact from the Professor. Why had he not followed up the clue that he must have been given by the Major? Did he really still believe the site was of no further interest? Something Sheila Snell had said had not rung true. He couldn't quite remember what it was.

He woke with a jerk. It was eight o'clock already and he was supposed to be dropping in on the party at Trent Road. He hurried out to his van, stopping at the telephone booth to find out which house he was supposed to be visiting.

CHAPTER 22

Professor Charleston

Trent Road, Hinkeaton, was a long uninteresting road, lined with nineteen-thirty semi-detached houses and sodium vapour lamps. In the damp December evening, the road surface shone like a river. It was the long road that has no turning, heading out of the town along what was presumably the river valley. The house he wanted was number 479, and he wonderd whether he would have any difficulty in identifying it. Presently he came to about a dozen cars parked close together. He drew in at the end of the line and extinguished his lights as the others had done. Opening the door he could hear the faint sounds of pop music. He walked over to the gate of the nearest house and confirmed that it was, indeed, 479. He walked to the front door through the dripping and neglected shrubbery and rang the bell. There was no reply so he knocked, heavily. The door was opened by a tall, thin, boyish looking man.

'I'm Peter Wood!' Peter shouted over the noise of amplified electric guitars.

'I'm Himself!' shouted the Professor, thrusting a large glass of red wine into Peter's hand. 'Come in and meet the gang.'

There were far too many people to meet for Peter to remember any names; Sheila Snell was there, dressed to kill in hot pants and little else. She was introduced as 'Snail Shell'. The other person Peter remembered as he was rapidly whisked around to meet the gang was introduced as 'Betty' and then, in hasty parenthesis, 'my wife'. He ensconced himself in a corner, feeling a bit out of place among these people who reminded him of some quotation. He thought for a bit, and then it came to him: 'What are these, so

159

withered and so wild in their attire, that look not like the inhabitants of the earth, and yet are on't?' He chuckled to himself as his mind raced on: 'You should be women, yet your beards forbid me to interpret that you are so.' Was that right? It didn't matter really. It was apt. He watched his host going around filling glasses. At first he looked, in the subdued light, quite the picture of the academic at home, in a well cut suit, with baggy knees and one button of his waistcoat missing. But whoever wore a sports shirt with patterned poinsettias in full colour, and matching tie, with a grey suit?

The Professor came around and refilled Peter's glass.

'I wanted to talk to you about an archaeological problem!' shouted Peter, hoping to find out something before both of them became befuddled.

'What the hell is that?' shouted the Professor.

'*À bas les archaeologists*!' shouted Miss Snell, grabbing Peter and dragging him into the middle of the room where she writhed provocatively in time to the music. 'Come on, dance, you great digging type!' she almost screamed.

Peter finished his drink quickly, and pocketed the glass, so that he could concentrate on what he was doing. This was what they called 'why dancing' when he was at university. 'Why dancing when you can stand right where you are and be wriggling?' they used to ask. When the music stopped, Snail Shell pointed up towards the ceiling. Too late Peter realised that he was under the mistletoe. She was on him. Not that he minded the experience. She might be a research assistant, he thought, but she's all woman. She didn't have any use for make up or perfume. He found himself wondering whether the scent of alcohol or perspiration was the more powerful aphrodisiac.

It was only a brief, but memorable, encounter. A game of musical chairs was suddenly organised. These college people must be a little weak in the head, Peter found himself thinking, when he and the Professor were fighting for the last chair. And he wondered how his glass had miraculously become full again. The party became more and more noisy and the games more childish as the evening went on. Then the lights were all turned off for a game of sardines, which ended in near panic as a large wardrobe collapsed, nearly crushing the people who had concealed themselves in it. Goodness knows how many, thought Peter, extricating himself and counting his limbs. What a pity I didn't find Snail Shell, he thought lecherously. Or come to think of it, he added to himself, returning to sanity, Charleston.

His search, when the lights had been put on and sticking plaster and sal volatile administered to the needy, failed to produce either the Professor or his charming assistant. He joined Mrs Charleston sitting at the bottom of the stairs, quietly killing a bottle on her own. She was a misfit, he thought. Quite the typical suburban housewife. She was still wearing her apron.

'Been washing up?' he asked.

'Someone has to do the mundane things. We can't always be his research assistants. We have to grow up sometime, more's the pity. What department are you from? We haven't met before, have we?'

'Actually, I'm not from the University at all. I came up to ask the Professor something about his work in Broadshire. I'm one of the dirt archaeologists from that County.'

'*That* County is just what you ought to call it,' she replied with unexpected bitterness. 'So close to London, and yet so uncivilised. I don't think Himself would like to go back. In fact, I don't think he wants to talk about the place any more. When he was down there doing that dig—what was the name of the place?'

'Water End.'

'That's it—Water End. Do you know some of your natives stole his car, with everything in it, just as he was about to come home? The police eventually returned it, but he wasted lots of time and energy on it, just when he was worn out anyway. Then take the last time he went down there. Supposed to be talking to a learned society in a civilised county town. Came in in the early hours all covered in mud. Lucky it was his old suit. The cuffs were all frayed anyway. I couldn't have faced sending it to be cleaned in that state. But you'd think in a civilised place they would have proper made-up roads, and proper drainage, wouldn't you? He never said what happened. Perhaps he stopped off to stretch his legs or something and fell in a ditch. I didn't ask. Just pitched his suit away. He never missed it.'

'I thought he might be interested in going back and finishing his work at Water End soon,' Peter observed.

'I don't think so. He wrote a final report, you know, for the Antiquaries. He has found another site in Buckinghamshire for his training and research programme now. Anyway, I just know that he hates the place. You can tell, you know.'

She poured herself a full tumbler of wine and drank it quickly.

'It must be difficult, keeping a professor well turned out to meet his fellow academics. Quite expensive, keeping good clothes well valetted, if that's the word, especially if the wearer is an archaeologist.'

Mrs Charleston was looking rather glazed, but was still able to follow the conversation.

'Expensive, keeping clothes and assistants on a professor's salary; and buying a house,' she complained.

'I suppose there would still be good wear in his old suit, for a tramp or down-and-out. What did you do with the old one?' He mentally crossed his fingers. It was a long shot.

'I used to be his—old one—you know. Exciting being a resist assearchment with an archaeolologist. Goo' mental and phys—physical exercise. Oh! His old suit? Put out for the Oxfam people. But you can't send it all muddy, even if it is charity. Anyway, you can't imagine the underprivileged refugee trotting around in a grey pinstripe. 'Spect it's still in that box in the garage. Don't worry. He won't find it.'

Her concentration wandered again.

'He's not here anyway. Taken that Snail Shell girl home. Exciting being a—one of them. I used to be one once. Useful exp—experience. Would you like to put me to bed?'

Peter gently took the glass from Betty Charleston's hand, and placed it carefully with the now empty bottle in a corner close to the wall. He picked up the lady and carried her upstairs. As he reached the top, he was passed by a young couple going down, and had to stand against the bannisters to let them past. They did not make any comment. He opened the door of the front bedroom, with some difficulty, and was pleased to find it unoccupied. He put his unconscious burden down on the bed and contrived to cover her with the eiderdown. Then he tiptoed downstairs. He made his way to the back door, pushing past a necking couple.

'A little fresh air,' he explained.

'I should do it on the rhubarb patch, if I were you old man,' said the man. 'Nitrogen and lots of phosphates is what rhubarb really likes best.'

Peter walked out of the back door of the Professor's house, and closed it after him. It was pitch dark at the back of the house, beyond the reach of the sodium vapour lamps in the street, and very quiet after the continuous din from the record-player. It was cold, too, and a light drizzle was falling. He stood and let his eyes become accustomed to the darkness. He turned towards the front of the house, moving stealthily. A garden tool on a long handle which had been left leaning against the wall of the house, caught him a smart blow across the shin, and slid slowly down the wall until it reached the ground. There was a sound like breaking flowerpots. He stood still, waiting to see if anyone had noticed the noise. Not with the din they were making themselves inside. He continued around the house until he came to the front of the garage, brushing against a broad-leaved evergreen which showered him with water, much of which went down his neck.

As he expected, the garage doors were open, and propped back by bricks. The doors faced the road and some light from the street lamps managed to filter that far. He wondered what he could possibly say to the Professor if that worthy came home and found him searching in the garage. He tried to think of something that he might legitimately want, and decided that he might say he wanted a spanner to tighten something in his own engine. Perhaps the Professor would believe him. As he made his way slowly into the garage, examining with the help of his lighter the accumulated junk of years piled high against the walls, he wondered how long Charleston might be. Did he just take Miss Snell home and return almost straight away, or would he be like the mills of God? Better assume the former, and get out as quickly as possible.

Still no box containing clothing. Boxes of almost anything else here: clothes pegs, car mats, Roman pottery, offcuts of wood ... here it was, behind this striped canvas object. He realised it would need both hands to lift the deck chair. He let the lighter snuff itself, and put it in his pocket. Grasping the chair with both hands, he pulled it towards him. A cascade of bottles and tins clattered onto the floor. He stepped forward and, with appalling swiftness and in utter silence, something hard, boney and very cold descended on the back of his neck. He let go of the chair, and found his arms pinioned to his sides. His heart pounded in his ears and he almost screamed aloud, until the explanation of the silent and murderous attack suggested itself to him. With hysteria fought down, he released himself from the prop which held the deckchair up when it was in use.

With great self-control he re-lit his lighter and examined the box he had discovered behind the diabolical chair. In it appeared to be clothing. He looked at the mess on the floor, and decided that he couldn't face the nervous strain of clearing it up, when his host might appear at any moment. Taking the box in both hands, he ran out to his van, showering himself with icy water from the shrubbery as he ran. Opening the door, he threw the box into the back and collapsed onto the driver's seat, trembling. If this was only petty larceny, heaven help the first-story men. They must die young. He wondered whether to go back, at least to get himself a drink to steady his nerves. He decided that he couldn't face it, and that there was no point if his host was away with the serving wench. A car came down the deserted road very fast indeed, swept into the drive and disappeared into the garage. He could hear the crunch of broken glass and deckchair under its tyres. He decided that he wouldn't go in, even if his host had returned. Making a quick note of the time and his milometer reading he set off for home.

CHAPTER 23

To talk of many things

Peter woke next morning from a deep dream of Sheila Snell. Lucky bastard, that Professor. Fancy having an assistant at all; to have one who undertakes other duties of a personal nature, and who is qualified for both jobs is just wonderful. He thought back over the events of the last evening. He had been all the way to Hinkeaton University to meet Charleston, and had exchanged only a few words with him. Perhaps what he had discovered was unimportant, but there was something not quite right about Charleston's attitude to the archaeology of Broadshire, as reported by his nearest and dearest. On the other hand, he meditated as he cooked his breakfast, it might be quite natural for an academic archaeologist to be uninterested in a place when he is not actually working there. It certainly seemed quite normal for the University to carry out an excavation virtually quarantined from the *hoi polloi*. What Major Forbes had actually asked the Professor at that meeting of the BAAAS, like the song the sirens sang, was not beyond conjecture, but it must be admitted to be a hypothesis. And certainly his motives for asking it were doubly hypothetical.

After breakfast, Peter made a number of telephone calls. The first was to Mrs Duguid.

'Good morning, Mrs Duguid. I'm lucky to find you at home, I expect.'

'Why indeed yes! Do you know, we are going to spend Christmas this year with our very good friend Sir Charles at Duntop Manor? He's such a dear man. A real baronet and, just fancy, a first class honours man at Cambridge as well! And the day after Boxing Day, we are off to join our tour. This year we are going to be shown round Palestine by Sir

Henry Spratt and Professor Emeritus Daniel Birch. Isn't it all too exciting!'

Peter butted in.

'What I phoned for was to ask your help as an expert,' he lied. 'I have been asked to visit your old friend Alan Charleston up at Hinkeaton. I was wondering if you knew any easy short cuts to get there. I don't want to take the van up in the winter. You never know, the weather might break. Anyway, I can get on with some work if I use public transport.'

'Well, we always go up in our big car, the Jaguar, and use the motorway. You can do it in about three and a half hours.' Peter had done it the previous night in three hours from door to door, but he held his peace. 'But dear Alan always comes down by rail. You don't have to go into London and come back out; there is a train which cuts across onto this line.'

'Thank you,' said Peter. 'I suppose that would be the way he came down to give the lecture at the BAAAS last summer?'

'That's right. Hubby met him at the station in the little car, the Vauxhall Viva. Must have been a very fast train too. He was there just as the train was due to arrive, and Alan was waiting for him. So you mustn't always complain about British Rail!'

'Thank you very much, Mrs Duguid; you don't know how much you have helped me. That sounds a wonderful service. I must try it.' He rang off quickly.

His next call was to County Police Headquarters. He asked to be put through to Ken Harris.

'Morning Ken! How's crime today?' he asked breezily.

'Quiet. And I hope that's how it's going to stay. I want none of your damned archaeological goings on, thank you very much. After that disastrous business of the Major's untimely end. I'm lucky not to be back pounding the beat. The Chief Constable was very nice about it, considering all things, but he really tore me off a strip. Not only did I go around on the enquiry with a sort of unsworn deputy—that's you; I explained you were an expert assistant—but I also went off half cock in deciding it was a case of homicide, telling all those influential people. Not one of my best efforts. And the file is still open, though we've nothing to put in it.'

'Can you drop round to see me this evening about eight?' asked Peter.

'Business or pleasure? Do I bring along a sergeant to take it down to be used in evidence, do I bring the 'cuffs, or do I bring a bottle with me?'

'Shall we say a busman's holiday? Don't bring along a uniformed sergeant, just the bottle will do. I'm asking Bill Denny over, so there is bound to be some call for liquid refreshment before the evening is done.'

'Righto then—see you about eight!' said the Inspector jovially and put down his receiver.

Bill Denny was only too pleased for a chance to come out for an evening's entertainment.

'What's happened, have you won the pools or something, old son?' he asked with a laugh.

'Nothing like that, Bill. I'm expecting a policeman to come for me tonight. I've come into possession of a rather interesting artifact, but it's not really my property.'

'Ah! Have you been digging on someone's land without permission?' asked Bill.

'I'll tell you about it when I see you. I'm afraid I've stolen a professor's trousers! Bye!' He put the receiver down.

That evening, the Inspector and the cabinet maker arrived together and were soon ensconced in front of the fire, with tankards in their hands. Peter explained to the Inspector, starting from first principles, about the field work that he and Bill had done near Water End, leading up to their conviction that the site that Professor Charleston had been working on was, in fact, the Pognemton of the Itinerary. He

168

did not explain why they had started the work in the first place.

'Fine bit of detective work. Lot of evidence accumulated. All circumstantial, of course,' the Inspector said, accepting a further libation and putting his feet up on the mantlepiece. 'I can't see why no-one has ever seen it before.'

'Oh, but they have!' said Bill. 'The farmer thought it was so well known as to require no explanation. And there was one other person who realised the possibility, but never got round to doing the leg work.'

'Who was that?' asked the Inspector.

'Fiercesome Freddie Forbes, no less,' replied Bill.

'He never told anyone, as far as I know,' said the Inspector.

'I think he did, indirectly. Do you remember that nearly everyone at that meeting of the BAAAS agreed on one thing,' said Peter. 'Forbes asked a question about Roman roads, and he seemed excited at the time. He'd just twigged on from internal evidence in Charleston's paper.' He explained about the bronze letters and the significant arrangement of the walls.

'I see,' the Inspector nodded agreement, 'and the Professor didn't twig it?'

'Either that, or he didn't want to admit it. I must say,' Peter went on, 'it seems very unlikely that Charleston didn't get the obvious inference, either then or later. What had occurred to us was that Charleston didn't *want* the inference to be drawn. We thought he might have wanted it kept secret for now, or something like that. However, I have found out that he has lost interest in the site completely.'

'You aren't suggesting,' squeaked Bill, 'that he had such a good reason for wanting the secret kept that he would do old Freddie in?'

'Let's say that I can think of a reason why he wouldn't want the idea to gain acceptance. It's a hypothesis at present, but it would be capable of experimental proof,' replied Peter.

'I'm afraid I would need much more to go on before I could possibly become involved again officially,' said the Inspector regretfully. 'It'd be more than my job would be worth to re-awaken the slumbers of the Forbes's file. What does your story amount to? You have done some fieldwork and established a good case for a particular site being documented and named in the Roman period. You find it surprising that the excavator didn't realise this possibility. You infer that Forbes must have thought it out, and that he threatened to let the cat out of the bag. You then suggest that the Prof had some good reason for not wanting the story to come out, and that he silenced Forbes, choosing the most unlikely time, place and method that anyone could dream up. He couldn't even have been there. He was on his way back home at the time.'

'How was he travelling back home?' asked Peter.

'He must have gone back by train,' answered the Inspector. 'We can deduce that, even if he didn't say so in his statement. Let me think.' He accepted another tankard of ale and stared into the fire. 'I was looking at the statements only the other day. Failure does rankle, you know. Ah! Got it! The Duguids said that they had to hurry their dinner so that they could bring the speaker in, yet they lost him at the end of the meeting. Since he travelled with them in their car, and didn't travel back with them, it follows that he would have been stranded in Broadchester without a car. It follows that he must have gone back by train. We did check up in other ways. There was a train at the right time; although no-one remembered seeing him on the station that night, there was a train at midnight and he did later collect his expenses, first-class return fare, from Doolittle-Smythe. Anyway, he was back at the University first thing in the morning—so there!'

He beamed triumphantly at his own feat of memory and deduction.

'Let me tell you a story,' said Peter, 'which might fit the facts that we know equally well. Suppose Charleston originally arranged to be met at the station by Mr Duguid. Or, on second thoughts, that Mrs Duguid arranged that he should be met. For some reason, connected with his work or something, he was prevented from catching the cross-country train which would get him to Broadchester on time. He decides to motor down. It can be done quicker by road, using the motorways, than by rail. I know, I did it last night in three hours, without being caught by the fuzz. With no ulterior motive at all, it would save explanations if he were to park his car at the station, and meet Duguid as arranged. Mrs Duguid did remark that Charleston met her husband early—implying that he might have arrived before the train was due.'

'It would fit the facts, but it's a pretty tenuous theory. And not likely to be capable of being checked at this late date—sorry,' said the Inspector.

'There are two people who have already supported my story,' said Peter smugly. 'The first is a Miss Snell, who assists the Professor in more ways than one. She says that he gave her a lift that day as far as Bedford. You don't give people lifts if you are travelling first class on the railway. Secondly, Betty Charleston, the Prof's wife, says that he probably got out to stretch his legs on the way home. You don't do that on a train. At least, not in such a way as to get your trousers all covered in mud.'

'Did he by jove! You've got me interested at last!' The Inspector sat up straight in the chair, with his eyes shining. 'Still, that only tells us that he could have been there.' He sat back.

'Suppose you had known about this possibility sooner, and had a sample of the mud from his trousers. Would that have been of any help?' asked Peter, innocently.

'Chance would be a fine thing,' retorted the Inspector. 'What do you think we are, Sherlock Holmeses or something? What sort of question can you ask a piece of mud?'

'In archaeology we might try to find its origin,' suggested Bill.

'There is a faint hope, I suppose, that you might compare it with a sample from elsewhere, and conclude that there was a probability that the specimens were identical. Not a very good probability. And you'd have to know what sample to compare it with.'

'You are thick tonight,' said Peter, rudely. 'I took you to the Villa the day after the body was found. What was the ground like at the time?'

'Dry as a bone,' replied the Inspector without hesitation. Then his eyes lit up again. 'Except at the stream,' he added.

'Right. Given time, you know, you might make a good detective,' chortled Peter.

'You wouldn't,' the Inspector said. 'Given a sample of mud from the suspect's trousers, we might be able to use it as supporting evidence. We haven't even got a suspect.'

'Never mind,' said Peter, reaching under his desk, 'at least we've got the trousers!'

Before he opened the cardboard box that he had taken from Charleston's garage, Peter gave a quick résumé of how he had come by it.

'It's just too much,' said the Inspector, bitterly. 'I bet no amount of leg work by my merry men would ever have produced such an unlikely piece of evidence. You realise that it is virtually useless. You took the box without permission, and there are no witnesses as to its provenance. And your mud is only a weak bit of evidence in itself. It might have a hundred different origins. Add to that the fact that Mrs Charleston would never give evidence against her husband, and we've only her story that they are her husband's trousers and that he wore them that day for the last time. Still, let's have a look. Just for us, not for a jury.'

They opened the box and took out a complete suit of

clothes, grey with a faint pinstripe. Jacket, waistcoat and trousers. The trousers were mudded up to the knees. The Inspector went through the pockets systematically and found only a couple of Midland Red bus tickets, and a dry cleaner's label fastened inside a jacket pocket with a safety-pin. He turned his attention to the trousers.

'We'd be able to get a fair sample of this mud for the lab,' he said. Then he looked more closely at the turn-ups. He carefully picked a small object from one of them. 'What do you think this is, Peter?' he asked, putting it carefully into Peter's open palm.

Bill half rose from his chair, and looked at the object. It was a curious flat seed, about an eighth of an inch long, almost trapezoid. The peculiar thing about it was that at two corners of the same edge, small spikes stuck out of it. These spikes were covered in minute barbs, like harpoons. It was these barbs which had been responsible for this seed and a number of others adhering to the cloth.

'I wouldn't know if I hadn't had them stuck in my own socks on a couple of occasions,' said Peter. 'These are the fruits of the bur marigold.'

He rose and went over to the bookcase on the far wall, returning with a thick volume. After a little searching, he read from the book: ' .... . Achenes flattened, crowned by two or three (rarely four of five) awns, with minute deflexed prickles. In wet ditches and marshes throughout Europe, Asia and America. Common in England.'

'O.K.,' said the Inspector. 'We've almost established to our satisfaction that he must have been in a marshy place or in a ditch—probably that night.'

'There was a lovely patch of bur marigold, alias *bidens cernua*, near the place where the footpath to Cold Beech Villa crossed the stream,' said Peter. 'It may *say* that it's a common plant, but that's the only local place that I have seen it. It is just another piece of confirmatory evidence. We're not going to put it to a jury, you know.'

'It's a lovely tale, old son,' said Bill, stretching. 'But as you say, can we prove anything?'

'I doubt it,' said Peter, 'but why not give it a try. I don't imagine that Ken here will want to get officially involved yet. He can get me some information without raising a hue and cry, though.' He turned to the Inspector. 'Let's pretend that this is just an academic exercise that we're doing. I promise not to give anyone outside this room a hint of what we're doing. Just let me follow this through for my own satisfaction. You can help by looking up a few details for me. Are you game?'

'I wish you wouldn't use that word,' said the Inspector. 'This isn't a game, and if you say the wrong thing in the wrong place, the least trouble you'll have is a slander suit filed.' He hesitated. 'Still, I'd like to be sure for myself, even if we haven't got a case to go to court. What do you want to know?'

Peter opened another bottle.

'There's one link in my chain that is even more tenuous than the others. It isn't last summer, but the one before. Could you find out for me what happened to delay Charleston's departure at the end of his dig at Water End? July it would have been. I understand that his car was pinched just before he was supposed to leave.'

'That's a detail I can check on without rousing anybody's blood pressure,' said the Inspector. 'Righto. Leave it to me. Anthing else you want to know?'

'What happened to the Major's papers after his death?' asked Peter.

'There's nothing for you in them. Don't forget, we had our own experts looking at them for clues.'

'I just wanted to have a look at the manuscript of the book he was supposed to be writing, that's all,' said Peter.

'That's easy. All his archaeological papers went to the Broadchester Museum. They were left to the BAAAS and Mr Bugg agreed to take care of them.'

CHAPTER 24

Just digging

There is a belief among armchair archaeologists that
summer and excavation must go together. In fact, the
general public are all aware that the best possible
archaeology is practised in regions where, if it is not true
that the sun never sets, it can be said that it is rarely
obscured during the day by clouds. The term 'archaeological' and 'dry-as-dust' have become synonymous.
So, almost everyone assumes, excavation is best
undertaken in the middle of a howling desert at the
height of the dry season. A very poor second best must be
any sort of digging in Britain. In such a backwater, where
there can be no imaginable time which might be called the
dry season, respectable archaeology is only possible in the
field during the months of July and August. This is the time
when the dons are able to cast off their academic fetters.
Perhaps the university year was designed with the needs of
the excavator in mind.

It is not quite everyone who assumes this state of affairs
to be natural law. The archaeologists who, like Peter Wood,
devote most of their time to the battle in the trenches—to
saving as much as possible of the past from deep ploughing
and the maw of the bulldozer—have had, when the Devil
has driven, to undertake their work in the most unlikely
situations and under conditions which might be thought to
be impossible to mere students of the art. They have
discovered that rain, snow and frost are not ideal conditions
but that they make the actual work inconvenient, not
impossible. The effect of fighting the elements for the prize
on the morale of the workers is, perhaps, not unexpected.
One might say that adventure is inconvenience anticipated

in tranquillity.

Peter had no difficulty, therefore, in obtaining a team of twenty volunteers to assist with 'a little stab at the landscape' in late January. He had no difficulty at all in whistling up, from somewhere, one of those enormous machines which are often to be seen on housing estates under construction—the great yellow monsters which look like a cross between a tractor and a mechanical grab. The biggest difficulty he had found was obtaining permission to dig where he wanted to. Not that the farmer minded. Mr Perryman was very pleased to allow the work to go on again in Tile Mead, Water End. The chief obstacle had been the Minister for the Environment, or rather the officials who served that Minister.

Once a site is recognised and defined, it is within the powers of this Minister, upon advice, to schedule the site as being an ancient monument. This process, while not actually providing the site with guardianship, does have the effect that it is, to a degree, protected. No-one can disturb the site, in theory, without the possibility of facing a small fine. In practice the law is, at present, largely ineffective and very few offenders are proceeded against. Nevertheless, if Peter was to go ahead with the use of machines on his project, it would be quite possible that he would lose favour with the Minister, who had taken his responsibility sufficiently seriously to schedule the Water End site.

It had required a little pulling of strings and a few words in the right ears to provide the necessary permission for his project. It had been a difficult negotiation because of the peculiar nature of his request. He had wanted to re-excavate part of a site which had recently been dug by one of the foremost experts of the day, but he had particularly required that the expert should not be consulted. And, of course, he had not been able to explain his reason for wanting to do the work.

Luckily, the inspector for the Department who was most

176

closely involved had turned out to be an old pupil of Peter's, and had been able to slip the project through without exciting too much interest. Peter had permission to excavate an area twenty-five yards square in Tile Mead, not too closely specified, at no specified time. He had undertaken that the findings would be reported in the *Transactions of the Broadshire Archaeological, Antiquarian and Architectural Society*, and to deposit any finds with the Broadchester Museum. Not that he expected that there would be any finds to deposit.

Acting on information received, as the expression is, Detective Inspector Kenneth Harris arrived at Perryman's Farm during a light fall of snow. He was surprised to see what appeared at a distance to be army manoeuvres. In place of tanks the army was using a large yellow tractor, and the regulation tin hat had been replaced on each of the men by a bright red polypropylene helmet. A roaring fire had been made, from which rose a column of grey smoke. Large heaps of black soil contrasted strongly with the white of the rest of the landscape. He followed the track from the farm right to the side of the excavation and saw that the group, although obviously purposeful and organised, were in anything but uniform. Each wore a regulation red helmet, with the letters BAC on them in yellow, and each wore rubber boots, but the rest of their clothing was varied, colourful and many-layered. Clearly they were assisting the machines to remove the topsoil to an accurately controlled depth, leaving very little loose soil in the hole. He spotted his friend Peter, who could be distinguished by a small Union Jack on a short pole which projected from his helmet. He was looking through a level, and making signs with his hand to a distant man with a staff.

Harris walked over to Peter, rather surprised to find that no-one took any notice of him at all. It was as if he were invisible. The machine continued its task, tearing up great mouthfuls of black soil, for all the world like a prehistoric monster at mealtime, gobbling up a diet of mud. Around it toiled the accolytes, keeping their area clean and tidy, and feeding any dropped crumbs back with shovels. In the background burnt a large fire of timber, from which the smoke rose almost vertically into the leaden sky. And the light snow floated downwards, sprinkling everything. It could have been a scene from one of those silly anachronistic films. The beginning of the Ice Age, complete with cave-men and bright yellow Jurassic amphibian. Peter was absorbed in whatever task he was doing. He glanced up and saw his friend.

'Just a tick, old lad.'

He wrote in a notebook, which he tucked inside his donkey jacket to preserve it from the weather. Then he shouted an instruction to the man with the staff.

'What on earth are you up to now?' asked the Inspector.

'Quick stab at the landscape,' replied Peter. 'We don't have any really urgent work on just now, and it pays to keep the old team up to scratch. You could call this an exercise for the troops; just exercise. We're not really digging for information in the usual sense; just doing a little checking on a theory of mine. All this chunk of landscape has already been gone over pretty thoroughly by a certain well-known university. Hence the JCB.' He waved his hand at the machine. 'We'll get this little lot off this afternoon, then we can do a little cleaning up. We finish the job tomorrow—the digger driver will be off then—and then the machine can backfill Monday morning. Sorry I can't stop; you can see we've got a pretty tight schedule. There'll be a cup of tea in a couple of ticks.'

'What are you digging for?' shouted the Inspector, as Peter started to walk over towards the scene of operations.

'Surely you can guess that, can't you? Information. I'll tell you what. I'm trying to arrange an extraordinary meeting of the BAAAS to discuss what we find. It'll be arranged pretty quickly, and you'll be invited as a guest.

178

Make sure you come. It should interest you.'

The Inspector stayed for tea. It came in large tin mugs, was very strong and sweet and contained alcohol. It was drunk round the fire. Tea break was a very social affair and he managed to have a chat with Bill Denny, who appeared to be something like a chargehand in the gang. No information was forthcoming about the reason for the excavation, however.

CHAPTER 25

The final lecture

Peter was true to his word. By some process which he did not explain fully, an extraordinary meeting of the BAAAS was called for February 14th. The invitation which he received told the Inspector that the purpose of the meeting was to receive a paper called 'Recent Work on the Antonine Itinerary in Broadshire', to be read by Peter Wood, BSc.

The Inspector took Peter to the hall used by the Society, which was the old Shire Hall, also used for the Assizes. Peter talked all the way about everything except the meeting. All he would say about that was,

'You'll enjoy it. Chances are I shall make a complete ass of myself and be completely ostracised by the County for ever after. I really shouldn't do it, I suppose.' But he wouldn't say what it was that he proposed to do.

When they arrived, the hall was already full, and the Inspector quickly realised that the people who were there were all people he had met before in the course of his duty, with the exception of three clergymen, one of them obviously a bishop. Perhaps Peter had arranged for only those who attended Major Forbes' last meeting to be present. As if to confirm this, he spotted Professor Charleston on the far side of the room. Peter insisted on re-introducing him. He then left them with the words 'Excuse me, I must go and arrange my slides with the projectionist.'

The Inspector could do nothing but exchange a few words with the Professor about the weather, and make a few rather non-committal remarks about the archaeology of the County, using material that he had gleaned during his acquaintance with Peter. He was quickly put out of his misery by the Lady Chairman bringing the meeting to order.

'I should like to call upon the Secretary to read the minutes, but he is, unfortunately, unable to be with us tonight.'

'I propose that we take them as read.'

'Seconded.'

'Are there any votes against the proposal that the minutes be taken as read? Carried *nem con*. I now call upon our speaker tonight to read his paper. Everyone here knows Mr Wood, I think. His paper is entitled "Recent Work on the Antonine Itinerary in Broadshire". Mr Wood.'

Peter began his lecture straight away with a slide. It showed the County in outline with the known, or reasonably certain, Roman road patterns. He then explained that, in fact, all the work that he intended to talk about was concentrated in one part of *Iter* XVII of the Itinerary, the part near Durford. With illustrations taken on the ground that winter, interspersed with a light-hearted commentary, he quickly went through the work that he and Bill Denny had done in the field. He had a quick, fluent delivery, and the slides were all well photographed and colourful. The Inspector could feel the audience warming to the speaker, hanging on his words. The tour along the alignment of the suggested road was concluded with a picture of the ford at Perryman's farm.

'This brings us to a really interesting conclusion, ladies and gentlemen. If I am right, then what we have been tracing in the field must be none other than the tenth stage of the seventeenth *Iter*. This stage goes, we are told, from Sestonium to Pognemton, a distance of six *mille passum*. The route has hitherto been assumed to lie under the present A7 road, which would make Pognemton the old name for Durford. Taking the same distance on the suggested re-alignment, however, brings us to Water End.'

The slide changed, revealing the old drawing of the house which had preceeded Perryman's Farm, and Peter explained how he and Bill Denny had come to see the picture, and the brief history of the farm. The next slide showed the back of the picture.

' .... and so, you can see, ladies and gentlemen, that the place name has remained, or at least did remain, only slightly altered until the end of the eighteenth century, when it unfortunately went out of use just too early to get incorporated into the tithe maps which are the earliest survey of the area.

'Now it may seem strange to you that no-one has previously realised that Pognemton and Water End were the same place. This is not true, in fact, as certainly the present farmer of the site has always assumed it to be common knowledge. It was certainly known to the last rector of the Parish who, unfortunately did not publish his findings.

'However, there was one other person who became aware of the fact, and who did intend to publish it, but was prevented by his untimely death.'

The slide changed and part of a typewritten page was projected. It was typed in double spacing, like a manuscript for the printer.

'The tenth stage of this particular route ran from Sestonium (the present Straw Hill) to Durford. The presence of Roman tiles in Durford Church and a number of discoveries from the Roman period, now to be seen in Letchbury Museum, confirm that this town, on the river Dur, must have been Pognemton.'

The paragraph had been heavily scored through in black ink, and written across it in firm longhand were the words 'Pognemton = Pog Nemeton. Site of temple at Water End? Confirm by excavation.'

'These were, I believe, the last words written by the late Director of Excavations to this Society, Major Forbes,' Peter went on. There was no change in his style of delivery at all, and each stage of his argument was still illustrated by a slide. 'He met his death in this well'—picture of the well at Cold Beech Villa—'death by drowning. However, I believe that he didn't just lie down in the water and drown. He was helped by the judicious use of carbon dioxide. This is a heavy, asphyxiating gas, which, from a fire extinguisher like this one, photographed at the Villa, would cause anyone in the well to collapse, and eventually to drown.'

The Inspector became aware that the person sitting next to him was rising and was about to push past. He laid his hand on the man's arm.

'Don't leave yet, Professor. I think you ought to hear the rest of this,' he whispered.

'I should like, if you will bear with me,' Peter went on, 'to examine your late Director's last movements. You will all remember that he came to a meeting of the Society and that he asked a question of the speaker at the end of the paper. The question he asked was about the Itinerary. What prompted him to ask the question? I think it was the result of two things seen in quick association—these letters, cut from sheet bronze, which are often described as "votive" since we find them on temple sites, their use being unknown, and this plan, showing recent excavations of Water End. Note the walls at the top corner. They could be part of a temple, like the one shown in the next slide. He realised the possible significance, knowing that the word *nemeton* was a sacred grove to the Celtic peoples. He didn't just blurt out his idea. He had a little esoteric joke with the speaker, asking about the tenth stage of the seventeenth *iter*, knowing full well that the speaker knew the stages by heart and would, in all probability, get the point. The speaker did not appear to rise to the bait.

'The Major seemed, we are told, very excited. Significantly, he asked one museum curator about the distribution of Roman religious objects, and suggested that he would have to make room for some more finds. He asked the Treasurer of the Society if he had enough money for another excavation. He had a long discussion with the speaker, and was one of the last to leave.

'We can imagine him going home and pottering about. Perhaps he typed some more of the book he was working on. He almost certainly wrote the words we have just seen, indicating that he intended to re-open Water End and discover, once and for all, if there was indeed a temple on the site. There was a full moon, and he decided to go for a walk. He left his house and walked down this road, through the hedge and across this field. It is easy to take this way, even in the dark, if you have done it before. The only difficulty occurs at the little stream. If you don't take the right line, you end up by getting your trousers muddy, and even carrying burs from this bur marigold here. In fact, we know that is just what happened to the man who followed the Major.'

There was complete silence in the hall. The Inspector could feel the Professor stiffen in his chair. Peter went on.

'For reasons which we need not go into here, the Major let himself into the Villa building and, fetching a ladder which was always concealed there, climbed into the well. The man who had followed him came along and quickly took away the ladder, and then tried to reason with the Major, perhaps suggesting some business arrangement or other, which the Major was not interested in. I cannot tell why he did it, but the follower fired—if that is the word— a carbon dioxide extinguisher into the well. It gave a layer of unbreatheable air sufficiently deep to cause the Major to collapse and drown.

'Had the murderer not been so clever, the death might have provoked comment but not enquiry. The air at the bottom of a well is often foul. Unfortunately, he put the ladder tidily out of sight, propped open one door and fastened back the double doors. This he did to provide a good draft of air to disperse the carbon dioxide. It would have excited much less interest had he replaced the ladder in the well and left the doors as they were.'

184

The speaker took a sip from the glass of water provided by the rostrum. The audience was still spellbound.

'The murderer then went back home. Exhaustive police enquiries failed to produce any apparent motive for the crime. The criminal breathed a sigh of relief. His secret was safe; no-one would, he imagined, stumble on the true motive. To anyone other than an archaeological field-worker it would not appear to be a motive at all. The Major was killed just to prevent him from digging at Water End.

'It was only by chance that I got the first clue. Why, you may ask, would anyone want to prevent an excavation? In July of the year before last, a certain motor car was reported to the police as being stolen, along with its contents. The car was found abandoned next day, with most of its contents intact. One brief case was missing. I imagine the thief was disappointed at the contents. Apart from the camera, which would fetch a bit of ready cash, the contents were useless. They were the complete record of an archaeological excavation.

'The director of the excavation made a foolish decision. He still had the black and white photographs of the work in progress, and could borrow slides taken during the dig by visitors. My next slide shows the Water End excavations carried out in January of this year, by the group which I direct. And the final slide shows, in black, the features found by my group and carefully surveyed and double checked. In red are the features on the excavator's original plan. The same features—but they are not in the right places. What he didn't want to have the Major find out was the simple fact *that he had made the whole thing up*.'

'But I didn't mean to kill him!' shouted the Professor.

185

CHAPTER 26

Debriefing

'Manslaughter,' announced the Inspector to Peter and Bill, as he took a sip from his tankard in the snug at the *White Hart*. 'Manslaughter. We'll never know what really made him go that far. If he hadn't been so upset by your lecturing technique that he made that verbal admission, as we say in the trade, we'd never have pinned anything on him at all. He really wanted to get it all off his chest, you know. The difficulty was getting him to stop long enough to caution him. I think that manslaughter was as good as we could hope for a verdict, don't you?'

Peter and Bill both nodded wisely. They had not attended the Assizes, apart from a brief appearance by Peter to establish the authenticity and accuracy of his plan of the Water End excavation. They had been busy, they explained to Ken, with a little matter of a mosaic floor that needed rolling up.

'You were quite right, you know, Peter.' Ken settled back in his chair. 'Your Professor realised what old Forbes was getting at right at the outset. He says that he cursed himself, but decided to cover up. The plans that he had made up to save his face after the theft of his briefcase were already made into blocks for printing in the Antiquaries Journal, and the text was with the editor, if not already typeset. How could he admit that he had missed such an obvious point? Then, after the meeting, while coffee was being served, the Major was going around dropping hints about beginning a new research excavation. He asked Doolittle-Smythe if he could have the funds, Petchy if he would be available to do the surveying, Miss Spratt if she'd come and take charge of the finds and Bugg if he'd have room for the finds. He even dropped hints to Bugg about the distribution of votive objects. Then he got round to speaking directly to Charleston in private and found out that the University had no further interest in the site. So he announced his intention of re-opening the site to confirm the existence of the supposed temple.

'After the meeting, Charleston "somehow missed" the Duguids—not that I blame him, and walked back to the station where he had left his car. He started to drive back to Hinkeaton, but his mind kept on going over the dreadful possibility that Forbes' new dig would reveal the inaccuracies in his reported measurements. What greater disgrace can you imagine for one of the leading exponents of field excavation and recording than to be shown up as a fraud?

'After a brief stop at one of the refreshment places on the motorway, he decided to go back. Forbes was apparently quite well-known for his habit of doing his writing when it was quiet—in the early hours of the morning. The Professor arrived at Gamekeeper's Cottage just before midnight, only to see the Major's upright figure walking away down the road. Without thinking, he says, he followed the Major. In the bright moonlight it was quite easy to do this, except at the little stream where, as we surmised, he blundered into the mud and picked up seeds from the local flora, all unwitting. He says that it would have been *infra dig*, somehow, to call after the Major, especially in the middle of the night.

'By the time Charleston reached the Villa, the Major had already taken off his trousers, shoes and socks, and was down the well. Charleston looked over the edge and then, acting on the spur of the moment, decided that this situation somehow gave him an advantage over the Major. He simply whipped the ladder up, and then started to reason with the trapped man. This, of course, was a great mistake. If the situation had been explained to the Major where he had

Also published by **MILTON HOUSE BOOKS**

Hunt for Danger
by Avon Curry

A trip to Blackpool to meet his fiancée's family sounds innocent enough but Vince Bernard, personable young night-club owner from Brighton, finds the prospect dutiful rather than pleasurable. Certainly he was besotted by beautiful, ex-showgirl Hazel, although there was something secretive about her, even mysterious . . . . an added attraction perhaps?

Soon after meeting her Uncle Bill and Aunt Ada, Vince comes across their boss, local tough guy Leroy Malcolmson and is 'warned off' his territory after he tries to buy a local dilapidated mansion with an eye half to pleasing Hazel and half to turning it into some sort of club.

But Vince is not the man to be threatened by anybody. No crook himself, his hot Italian blood is stirred by the scent of trouble and disturbed by some indefinable threat to Hazel.

Hunt for Danger . . . . Vince smells it out, cannot resist it even though it seriously threatens not only his own life but also that of the girl he adores.

Avon Curry lays an exciting trail of violence and adventure in territory which, although set in the North of England is universal: the underworld of gambling, smuggling and law bashing; hunting, being hunted – and sometimes killing.

224 pages   **£2.30 net**